SHERMAN'S
LAST ROUND-UP

THE WORKS OF DAVID SHERMAN

SHORT FICTION
After Punk
In All Their Glory
Trouble On the Water
So It Begins
By Other Means
In Harm's Way

NOVELS
THE NIGHT FIGHTERS
Knives in the Night
Main Force Assault
Out of the Fire

A Rock and a Hard Place
A Nghu Night Falls
Charlie Don't Live Here Anymore
There I Was
The Squad
The Junkyard Dogs
The Hunt

DEMONTECH
Onslaught
Rally Point
Gulf Run

STARFIST
(WITH DAN CRAGG)
First to Fight
School of Fire
Steel Gauntlet
Blood Contact
Technokill
Hangfire
Kingdom's Swords
Kingdom's Fury
Lazarus Rising
A World of Hurt
Flashfire
Firestorm
Wings of Hell
Double Jeopardy

STARFIST: FORCE RECON
(WITH DAN CRAGG)
Backshot
Pointblank
Recoil

STAR WARS
(WITH DAN CRAGG)
Jedi Trial

SHERMAN'S
LAST ROUND-UP

DAVID SHERMAN

Pennsville, NJ

PUBLISHED BY
Paper Phoenix Press,
An imprint of eSpec Books LLC
Danielle McPhail, Publisher
PO Box 242,
Pennsville, New Jersey 08070
www.especbooks.com

ISBN: 978-1-956463-45-3
ISBN (eBook): 978-1-956463-44-6

To our knowledge, all of the stories in this collection, with the exception of "T'ain't Proper Grass Around Here" and "The Witch of El Paso," are reprints.

Copyediting: Greg Schauer
Cover Art and Design: Mike McPhail, McP Digital Graphics
Interior Design: Danielle McPhail, McP Digital Graphics
Calligraphic Design Elements © Anja Kaiser, www.fotolia.com

To the memory of David Sherman,
who was ready to set aside war and
have some fun with his writing.

We're sorry you had so little time to play.

CONTENTS

GREATER CRATER GREMLINS

CAPTAIN PEQUOD OF THE ARGUS, FLAGSHIP OF THE NEO-Butterfield and Overland Line, checked the lights on the command board to verify that everything was in readiness, before speaking into the brass funnel of the voice pipe to engineering.

"Mr. McCoy, release the brakes and wind the windlass."

"Release the brakes and wind the windlass, aye, captain," the chief engineer answered. With deft movements born of long practice, he maneuvered the levers that pulled the chains, releasing the chocks on the eight wheels on which the landship rode. He trod on the pedal that signaled the pusher team to transfer angular momentum from the flywheel to the massive propellers mounted above the stern of the landship.

Aft, the giant blades began spinning inside their anti-bird cages, slowly at first, but quickly picking up speed.

The *Argus* eased from her berth. Once she was at a safe distance, Captain Pequod spoke into the tube to the boiler room.

"Mr. Fletcher, do we have full steam?"

"We have full steam, aye, captain," the boiler officer replied.

"Then engage drive shafts."

"Engage drive shafts, aye, captain," Fletcher replied. He nodded to his chief petty officer, who tapped the boiler room's rating on the shoulder.

The rating, already firmly gripping the driveshaft control lever, put his entire weight into pulling the lever to the "engage" position. He was big enough and strong enough that the chief didn't have to help him, which the chief greatly appreciated.

Driveshafts engaged, the six drive wheels added their turning to the pushing of the propellers. The *Argus* quickly picked up speed, soon moving across the hardpan in the direction of Tombstone, Sonora Territory, faster than a horse could gallop.

Cheyenne Walker stepped onto the aft promenade deck and looked at the city the *Argus* was leaving behind. He was relieved to see no sign of pursuit. Of course, that didn't mean a message wasn't being wired ahead. Still; "I never thought I'd be so happy to leave Wichita," he murmured.

"The times they are a changin', Gamblin' Man," a feminine voice said behind him.

Walker spun about, the tails of his frock coat whipping about to slap his thighs, the derringer hidden in his sleeve slid into his hand. "Who's that?" he demanded.

"They call me Kitty Belle," the woman said, stepping from the shadows.

"Ma'am," Walker said, tipping his hat. He used the motion to slip his derringer back into its holster. "You sure did startle me there. Thought I was alone."

Kitty Belle's eyes crinkled with a smile; she'd noticed Walker's firearm. She fluttered a fan in front of her face to conceal the smile.

"That's what happens when you don't look," she said, taking a few sashaying steps in his direction. "You know who I am. So, who are you?"

"Ma'am, I am *so* sorry." This time Walker didn't simply tip his hat, he swept it off and bowed deeply. "I am known as Cheyenne Walker.

"'They call me,' 'I am known as,' Why, a body might think we aren't giving our real names!" she said with a tinkling laugh. This time she didn't conceal her smiling face.

Walker gave a shy smile. "Even my mother calls me Cheyenne Walker."

"Do tell," Kitty Belle said, taking the final step that placed her next to him at the promenade's railing. She seemed to also study the receding city.

Walker took advantage of the woman's rearward gaze to examine her. Green eyes and ivory complexion. Her lips looked to be naturally rosy rather than painted. He'd say on the short side of thirty, but not by much. Her crown reached his brow, but that was likely because her shoes had heels that added an inch or two to her height. A quick glance downward told him that was so. Her powder blue, sateen skirt was fashionably short, not quite ankle length. She'd left off what was surely a matching jacket in deference to the mid-summer Kansas heat, and left her blouse unbuttoned far enough to show just the edge of the cleft between her breasts. The beginning of dark circles under her arms made him wonder how long she'd been on deck before he'd come up. Altogether, sweat stains or no, a fetching appearance.

A slight smile creased Walker's face. He knew that he was a comely enough man, with just enough of an aura of danger about him, that many women found him nearly irresistible. He glanced at her left hand; no ring. Yes, *Miss* Kitty Belle might become a very agreeable companion between now and Tombstone.

Kitty Belle, for her part, smiled a secret smile; she was well aware of his examination. Cheyenne Walker didn't notice, even though she didn't use her fan.

Three smallish creatures hunched atop the landship's pilot-house, looking toward the disappearing city. One gleefully washed his hands one over the other as the second bounced joyfully on his haunches. The third's eyes glowed with malevolent elation.

"Soon, my friends, soon," the hand washer cackled. He looked to his left, at the setting sun.

"Soon, Grimblelich, soon," agreed Spindlebrake, the haunch-bouncer. He slashed at the air with curved talons.

Malevolent Eye didn't speak any more than he bothered with a name. He chortled in anticipation.

All three creatures turned their heads toward the setting sun, and watched as it ponderously dipped below the horizon. Then they rose and padded away softly, each in his own direction. They were half a day from Wichita—the *Argus* would soon be far enough from help.

It was the dinner hour on the *Argus*, and Captain Pequod invited Miss Kitty Belle to join him at his table. Not that she was the only person so graced. But Cheyenne Walker was not so invited. Instead, he found himself dining with First Officer Ishmael. The *Argus's* first officer was *not* a good conversationalist. Which was just as well with Walker; he was more interested in Miss Kitty Belle, and he spent the meal casting discrete glances toward the Captain's table—and the lady with whom he'd so recently become acquainted.

Dinner was soon enough over, and the captain gave the appropriate apologies to his guests before taking his leave to attend to his evening duties. "A captain's work is never done," he explained, "even on a landship." Cheyenne Walker took a long stride toward the captain's table, but had to abruptly change course, as Kitty Belle left the table without so much as a coy glance in his direction. He followed her. To the first-class salon as it turned out.

Before the evening ended and they retired to their separate cabins for the night, Kitty Belle had occasion to tap Cheyenne Walker on the nose with her folded fan and exclaim, "Why, Mr. Cheyenne Walker, what kind of girl do you think I am, sir?" She tittered, and tapped his nose a second time. Then, raising up on her toes, she kissed that nose tip before spinning gracefully and rushing off without a backward glance.

"I think you're *exactly* that kind of girl," Cheyenne Walker whispered once she was far enough away. He smiled as he headed to the bar for a nightcap before going to his cabin.

The next evening, Kitty Belle batted her eyelashes and convinced Captain Pequod to invite Cheyenne Walker to join them at his table.

Soon after sunset of the second day, the creature called Grimblelich wended his way through ventilation shafts, scuppers, and other hidden spaces, to the pilot house. There, using shadows when he couldn't keep objects between himself and where Helmsman's Mate Crusher, the lone crewman on duty, nodded in half-sleep, he crept to the gimble-mounted compass box.

At a soft snore from Helmsman Crusher, Grimblelich popped his head up to look into the compass box. Careful to not make a noise, he removed a lodestone from a pouch at his belt, slipped his fingers around it, and placed the backs of those fingers against the bowl of the compass box five degrees clockwise from where the compass was pointed. He then, oh-so-carefully, lifted and moved the compass circle, turning it three degrees counter-clockwise.

Risking another quick look at the sound of another snore, he nodded in satisfaction as his ploy worked; the needle moved from its previous position to that of the lodestone he held.

Grimblelich snickered, and slapped his free hand over his mouth to stifle the laugh that tried to burble up when an alarm chimed. He opened the fingers that held the lodestone and silently slipped it from his hand to the bottom of the bowl of the compass box, then hied himself to a hiding place.

Startled by the alarm, the helmsman's mate jerked erect and looked quickly around to determine the problem. The alarm chimed again in a specific sequence of dings and pings. The mate shook his head to clear the last of the nap's cobwebs, and stood over the compass box. He shook his head again, wondering how the *Argus* could possibly have veered eight degrees off course, adjusted the trim on the wheel, and watched as the bow of the mighty landship made its ponderous swing back to the course indicated by the compass needle. Once the *Argus* had resumed its course, the mate resumed his seat and nap.

Never once did he look out at the stars.

Twice more, Grimblelich caused the compass needle to move clockwise. The second time, he didn't wait for the alarm to chime before he affixed the lodestone to the bowl of the compass box. He knew that this time the navigator's mate wouldn't go back to sleep. Besides, he had another chore to do. The new direction of the *Argus* didn't need to be as precise as the old direction. They were now headed more westerly than they had before. Time enough for more exact aiming later.

Grimblelich headed for the boiler room, where he found a cubby and hunkered down to watch and wait for his next opportunity.

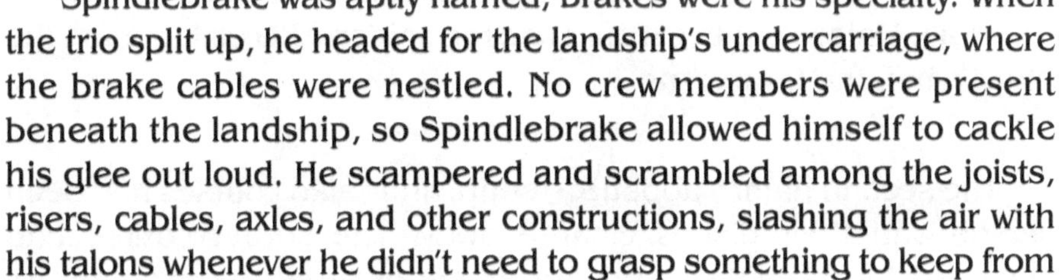

Spindlebrake was aptly named; brakes were his specialty. When the trio split up, he headed for the landship's undercarriage, where the brake cables were nestled. No crew members were present beneath the landship, so Spindlebrake allowed himself to cackle his glee out loud. He scampered and scrambled among the joists, risers, cables, axles, and other constructions, slashing the air with his talons whenever he didn't need to grasp something to keep from falling to the ground below.

Cackling, swinging, and scrambling, Spindlebrake traversed the length of the undercarriage from end to end, side to side, locating all of the brake cables, and following them from where they attached to the brakes to where they disappeared into the body of the landship. Once he knew what was what and where was where, he began slashing at the brake cables. Not quite enough to cut through them, but hard enough to affect them as he wanted. The damaged brake cables would last until the first time the brakes were applied after the landship stopped and started again. Until that time and no longer.

Spindlebrake was *very* good at what he did.

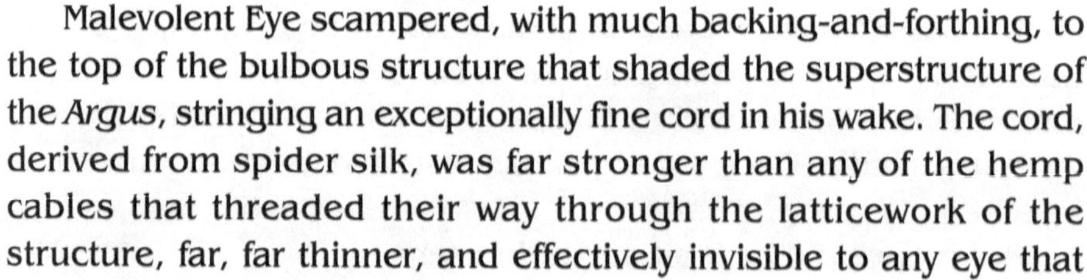

Malevolent Eye scampered, with much backing-and-forthing, to the top of the bulbous structure that shaded the superstructure of the *Argus*, stringing an exceptionally fine cord in his wake. The cord, derived from spider silk, was far stronger than any of the hemp cables that threaded their way through the latticework of the structure, far, far thinner, and effectively invisible to any eye that didn't know to look for it.

The latticework, up which Malevolent Eye scampered, was home to a series of precisely positioned mirrors, which funneled sunlight down to the boiler room in the bowels of the *Argus*. *It provided the heat to make the steam that propelled the mighty wheels on which the huge landship rode. The hemp cables that ran from mirror to mirror were used to shift the angle of the mirrors as needed to catch the sun's rays—or to turn from the sun to cease powering the landship.*

At each mirror Malevolent Eye inserted a plug, also derived from spider silk. The plugs were hollow vessels, filled with a glue that would turn to a granite-like hardness instantly upon being exposed to the air. Malevolent Eye would use the spider-silk cord to open the plugs when the time came.

The second night's appetizer, soup, and salad courses had been served and their dishes cleared away. The sorbet course had cleansed their palates, and the diners awaited the momentary serving of the chicken course, when the steward entered the dining room, unexpectedly empty-handed, and leaned close to whisper into the captain's ear.

Captain Pequod's face showed no expression as he listened, but he wasted neither time nor motion rising to his feet once the steward had delivered his message.

"I must beg your pardon," the captain said to his dinner companions, "but a matter has arisen that requires my immediate attention." With that, he departed the dining room.

Walker didn't notice any words exchanged, but First Officer Ishmael, Chief Engineer McCoy, and the other officers assembled in the dining room also rose and left. A mild buzz of curiosity spread throughout the dining salon at the departure of the landship's officers, but it quickly died down as the passengers returned to their meals.

"Whatever do you think might be the matter?" Miss Kitty Belle asked, her mascaraed eyelashes batting as her hand fluttered at her throat.

Walker slowly shook his head. "I surely don't know," he said as slowly as his headshake. "But in my many travels, I've never known it to be good when the captain and his officers were called from dinner."

Half an hour before Captain Pequod was summoned, a petty officer supervised three able-bodied landsmen in shutting down the shallow-draft day-boilers and switching over to the huge night-boiler, which had spent the entire day heating its water to a temperature that, kept under the correct pressure, would provide steam to keep the *Argus* under weigh all night.

Grimblelich watched with amused interest, and only once had to flop a hand over his mouth to keep a laugh from escaping. He had been on his job for a long time, and had acquired a level of patience that allowed him to watch so quietly, a trait which his companions in mischief didn't possess. That was why Spindlebrake and Malevolent-Eye had initial assignments that took them to places where nobody could spy them.

What with being well experienced at their jobs, and wanting their own dinners, the able-bodied landsmen changing over the boilers from day to night finished the job in short order, and it wasn't long at all before Grimblelich was left alone.

Again, here Grimblelich's experience came into play; he knew that one member of the boiler crew would rush through his dinner and return, so as to minimize the amount of time the boilers were left. And Grimblelich knew that sometimes the crewman would bring his dinner back to the boiler room (in violation of the rules) to further shorten the unattended time.

Grimblelich scampered from his cubby and pushed a chair under the bulge of the boiler. He clambered up the chair until he could reach a seam. From somewhere on his person he extracted a wooden mallet, from somewhere else a narrow, wood-handled chisel. With three blows that strangely failed to make the boiler ring with even a dull thud, he removed a stretch of weld-beading as long as it was high.

Grimblelich returned the mallet and chisel to their recesses and jumped off the chair, which he quickly shoved back to its place. From yet another place on his person he withdrew a grinder. He slithered under the parabolic mirror and began to grind the mirror's underside. The mirror reflected the sunlight that was drawn down and focused by the mirror-and-magnifier array from far overhead to the boiler room. He stopped before grinding all the way through. After returning the grinder to its hiding place, he withdrew a whisk and dustpan to clean up the shavings and dust he had created.

After a quick glance around to make sure he wasn't leaving anything behind, Grimblelich departed the boiler room by the same route he had entered. Now he allowed himself to laugh out loud. Several thin streams of steam already shot from the shaved seam, causing the boiler to lose pressure. The weakening of the mirror wouldn't be discovered until the next day when sunlight was again focused on it.

It wasn't long after the crewman on watch returned from dinner that he discovered the loss of boiler pressure.

Captain Pequod glowered at the leaking boiler. Until that split seam was repaired, the *Argus* wouldn't have nighttime power for its drive wheels. He shook his head. The situation wasn't as bad as it could be—the *Argus* was fully victualized, and she'd lose less than half a day's time. Still...

"Do you have any idea how this happened, Mr. Fletcher?" Pequod asked the boiler room officer.

"None, captain," Lieutenant Fletcher said. Confusion showed on his face. "We inspected the systems very thoroughly before we cast off from Wichita." He looked at the boiler chief for confirmation.

"Aye, skipper," Chief Scotty said. "We went over every inch of the systems, both of us! Everything was shipshape!" A scowl suggested that the chief knew something, but Pequod didn't ask about it.

"How long will it take to repair the boiler?" Pequod asked.

"We've got most of the pressure bled off," Scotty said. "Then we have to drain the beast to below the affected area before we can repair the seam. After that, the welding should go quickly. Unless something else goes wrong." He looked suspiciously around the boiler room. "It'll be ready to build pressure in time to give us full power for tomorrow night."

"Very good. I will leave you to it." The captain took his leave.

When he resumed his place at dinner, Captain Pequod shrugged off all questions about what had called him and his officers away with a not-quite brusque, "It was a minor matter of no particular consequence," and would say nothing more. The other officers were no more forthcoming.

The captain hurried through the remainder of his dinner, then arose and, with even less explanation than earlier, took leave. The other officers quickly followed. As did many of the passengers, some looking quite concerned. In a few short moments, Cheyenne Walker and Kitty Belle were among only a few passengers remaining in the dining salon, and the only ones at the captain's table.

"Could you hazard a guess as to what transpired this evening?" she asked, looking toward the doorway through which the captain and officers had disappeared.

He slowly shook his head. "No, ma'am, I would not care to do so." He looked at the same place. But he was certainly thinking about it.

"I suspect that a 'minor matter of no particular consequence' would be insufficient to call the captain and his officers from their dinner," she said after a moment.

He nodded as slowly as his earlier headshake. "I suspect you're right," he said. Then sat bolt upright. "Would you care to join me in the first-class salon for a cordial?"

"Why, Mr. Cheyenne Walker, how did you ever know what I was thinking!"

This evening, rather than tapping the point of his nose with her fan and asking what kind of girl he thought she was, Kitty Belle allowed Cheyenne Walker to escort her to her cabin. Standing in its doorway, she rose on her toes to brush his lips with hers before stepping back and closing the door on him. As soon as she heard him step away, she opened it a crack.

"Mr. Walker," she said through the narrow opening, "in Tombstone, I will be staying at the Oriental Hotel. Do come calling."

Walker grinned. "I will," he said. "You can be sure of that."

There was a bounce in his step as he returned to his cabin.

The bounce, however, died as soon as he closed his cabin door and his movements became brisk and purposeful. He opened his trunk and withdrew a flat box from its bottom. The box contained a Colt Buntline Special. The twelve-inch barrel made it impractical to carry unless he had a real need for its .45 caliber power, but there was something very wrong happening on the *Argus*, and he wanted to be prepared. He whipped off his frock coat and vest and strapped on his holster. He positioned it so that he could reach the butt of the pistol through the left arm hole of his vest. With his outer garments back on, he practiced drawing his pistol until he was sure he could draw it quickly, if needed. Armed and ready, he had one last thing to do. He dove back into his trunk for a brandy flask. He took a swig, and sloshed it around inside his mouth before spitting it out into the wash basin. Then a couple of splashes onto his face and frock coat and he was ready. He headed for the first of the places he thought Captain Pequod might have gone to when his dinner was interrupted.

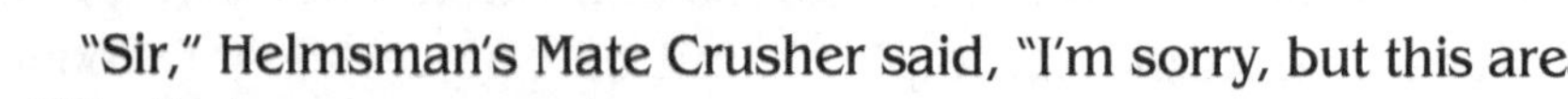

"Sir," Helmsman's Mate Crusher said, "I'm sorry, but this area is off limits to passengers."

"Ah, beg yer par'on," Cheyenne Walker slurred. "Whoa is thi' place if'n iss off limits?"

"Sir, this is the pilot house. We direct the landship's passage from here." Crusher stood to face the intruder.

"Zat so? An' how'd'ja do thet?" Walker stumbled as he took a couple of more steps into the pilot house.

"Please, sir," Crusher said, stepping in front of Walker, "you have to leave."

"Ever'thin' awright heah?" Walker asked.

"Everything's fine, sir. Now if you would kindly..." Crusher indicated the door.

"Tha's the way?"

"Yes, sir."

"Ah righ', I'll go."

Walker staggered and hummed off key until he was out of sight of the pilot house. Straightening up, he headed for the boiler room.

"I do declare," a soft voice said from a shadowed recess in the passageway.

Cheyenne Walker spun toward the voice and had his Buntline Special drawn and aimed before he recognized the voice.

"Miss Kitty Belle?"

"Why, so I am," she said, stepping from the deep shadow into the half-light of the passageway. "That is a powerful weapon for a gambling man," she went on, extending a finger alongside the barrel of the revolver and pushing it to the side, pointing away from her.

Realizing what he'd just done, Walker hastily put the revolver back into its holster, muttering an apology as he did so.

"I must needs wonder how a gambling man happened to come by one of Mr. Buntline's special Colts," Kitty Belle murmured, just loudly enough for Walker to hear. "I thought he had only a few made, for certain lawmen. More to the point, what are you doing creeping about below decks? And drinking!"

He ignored her question of how he got one of the fabled pistols but answered the others. "I haven't been drinking. I splashed some on me so I'd smell of brandy when I act drunk." He cocked his head at her. "And I imagine I'm skulking about below decks for the same reason you are—because something is amiss on the Argus and I intend to find out what.

"But what is a delicate lady such as yourself doing carrying a Colt Peacemaker?" he said as he quickly thrust a hand inside her short jacket, and grabbed the revolver he saw stuck in the left side of the waistband of her skirt, ready for a quick cross-body draw.

She pursed her lips and stared deeply into his eyes for a moment before saying, "Sir, I will thank you to remove your hand from my person and my belongings."

Walker slowly withdrew his right hand from where it rested on the grip of her pistol and slid his left hand onto the opposite side of her waist. "And what have we here?" He jerked his hands back before she could grab them, holding onto the object he'd found with his left. He held it high when she reached to snatch it away. It was a wallet, which he flipped open.

"Give that back right now!" Kitty Belle snarled.

Walker looked from the wallet to her—and the revolver she held pointed at his belly.

He gasped. "You're a Pinkerton agent?"

Cheyenne Walker hadn't expected whoever might be coming after him to already be on the Argus, much less to be such a fetchingly beautiful woman. He returned her identification wallet and they quickly discussed the situation. They agreed that something was dreadfully wrong on the *Argus*, and they needed to find out what it was. She also agreed not to arrest him before they reached Tombstone. For his part, Cheyenne Walker thought that gave him just enough time to figure out how to make his getaway.

Chief Scotty was in the boiler room, keeping a suspicious eye on the boiler—and every potentially suspicious shadow.

"Aye, and what do you want, Missy?" he snarled when Kitty Belle flounced her way into the boiler room, looking about with an expression of delighted discovery.

"Why, what do I want, sir?" she trilled. "I want to know it all! What is this place with all these marvelous noises and wonderful machines? What are their workings? What is their purpose in the

Argus? And," she stopped her tripping about and laid the tips of her fingers on his chest, "who are you, you wonderful man, who seems to be in command of all of this nigh magical domain?" She maneuvered so that Chief Scotty had to turn his back on the entrance to the boiler room if he was going to keep looking at her. And to make sure he would, she had undone the top three buttons of her blouse before entering. Chief Scotty couldn't help but notice the small triangle of female flesh thus exposed and turned as Kitty Belle wished.

Cheyenne Walker took advantage of the chief's distraction to slip into the boiler room. He had no idea of what to look for, but simply supposed that he would recognize anything that was out of place. Not that he knew what was *in* place in a boiler room, but he had to try.

And crouching so he wouldn't be seen if Chief Scotty suddenly turned around, he *did* see something out of place. The underside of the parabolic mirror that focused sunlight on the main boiler had been shaved so thin that Walker could see through it as he would a translucent glass. It took him no time at all to suspect that the shaving hadn't been seen by anyone in the boiler room's crew because they hadn't looked under the mirror. But what did it mean? On the other hand, was the thin spot on the mirror actually out of the ordinary? Cheyenne Walker wasn't an engineer and knew almost nothing about solar-powered boilers. Quickly satisfied that he'd discovered everything he could, he crept back into the passageway without being seen.

"Well?" Kitty Belle asked several minutes later, when she'd finally left Chief Scotty and she and Walker had retired a safe distance away from the boiler room.

"I don't know if it signifies anything," he said, "but it looked like someone recently shaved down the underside of the main mirror, the one that reflects the sunlight onto the boiler.

She thought for a moment, then gave her head a brisk shake, tossing her curls. "I don't know, either," she admitted. "And it's not something we can inquire about, because we'd have to explain how we came to see it." She shook her head again, dismissing the shaved mirror for the moment. "Where else do you think we should look?"

"I'd like to look at the undercarriage," Walker said. "But I suspect it's too dark down there now for us to see anything, and it might be too dangerous to light a Lucifer."

She looked at him questioningly. "Why would a Lucifer be too dangerous?"

"Not only a Lucifer, but any flame. There might well be solvents or other combustibles down there."

"Ahh." Kitty Belle considered the situation. "The mirror. If that *is* meaningful, there might be something in the array of mirrors above. What do you think?"

"I was beginning to think exactly that myself, ma'am. Follow me."

"Not 'After you'?" she asked coquettishly.

He slowly shook his head. "A man doesn't send a woman into danger first. He leads the way."

She smothered a laugh. But followed his example; Cheyenne Walker had his hand on the grip of his Buntline Special and Kitty Belle had her hand on her Colt Peacemaker.

An hour later they huddled in deep shadows near the base of the latticework tower that carried the array of mirrors high above the landship. Because of the darkness of the night, they'd had to search more by touch than by sight. That was how they'd been able to find the gossamer-fine, incredibly strong threads that led from mirror to mirror.

"They don't belong there," Cheyenne Walker whispered.

"Obviously," Kitty Belle agreed. "So, who put them there?"

His head shake went unseen in the darkness. "All I can say is, I disbelieve it was the crew."

"The damage to the mirror that you saw must somehow be related to these threads."

"I do believe you're right. I don't know exactly how the mirrors work, but I strongly suspect that when the focused sunlight hits that mirror, it'll burn straight through."

"And I believe *you're* right."

"You're the detective, what do we do about it?"

One thing they were certain of; they couldn't go to Captain Pequod with what they'd found. Too many questions would be asked about who they were, questions they didn't want to answer.

They agreed to sleep on it and see if their dreams came up with a solution.

Malevolent Eye almost never used words. He considered them as unnecessary as names. So when he went to Grimblelich with what he'd seen, he communicated with gestures, facial expressions, and a few grunts and other vocalizations, none of which could properly be called words.

Grimblelich caught the drift of Malevolent Eye's report.

"Then what did they do?" Grimblelich asked.

Malevolent Eye pantomimed that the two humans returned to their cabins, presumably to sleep without notifying Captain Pequod about the threads they'd found.

Grimblelich thought matters over for a few moments, then decided, "We must move our timetable up."

Malevolent Eyes glowed with elation.

Cheyenne Walker woke early the next morning. He arrived at the dining salon the same time as Kitty Belle. They were the first passengers to arrive, and the stewards were still setting up the tables for breakfast. Kitty Belle batted her eyelashes and smiled sweetly. They were allowed to seat themselves at a table against the wall, out of the way of the dining salon staff.

"Did you come up with anything?" Walker asked.

"No," Kitty Belle said with a shake of her head.

He looked unfocused at the entrance. "I think we have to tell the captain."

She shook her head sharply. "Captain Pequod would rightfully want to know why a woman passenger is exploring problems on his landship. And when he learns that I'm a Pinkerton agent, he'd believe that he would have to clap you in irons as a fugitive from justice. We have to deal with the problem ourselves. Besides, passengers aren't supposed to be carrying firearms on board the landship. So, *we* have to find out who is doing what."

"Or *what* is doing something." Walker looked away from the entrance and swept the entire room with his gaze.

Kitty Belle tilted her head. "'What'?" she asked. "Do you suspect it might be something supernatural?"

"Have you ever heard of gremlins?"

"Gremlins? You mean the little beasties that some people say cause mischief in airships?"

"The very ones." He looked at her with a serious expression. "You sound like you don't believe in gremlins. But I saw them once. I was on the *City of Angels*, flying from Seattle to Yerba Buena. Gremlins tried to make her crash. Only quick action by the captain and flight crew saved the airship and her passengers."

"You're serious."

"Very serious."

"What did the gremlins look like?" she asked, doubt tingeing her voice.

"Sort of like monkeys, but without the tails or the bellhop caps. And they moved twice as fast; they were almost impossible to shoot."

"Did you hit any of them?"

He shook his head. "Not from lack of trying." He looked off to the side. "But I've been working at improving my shooting ever since. Just in case."

She sat back and nibbled on her lower lip while she thought about what he'd just said.

Her reverie was interrupted when a steward arrived to take their breakfast order. They both requested steak, fried eggs, melon cubes, and coffee. They were halfway through their breakfast, with other diners just being seated, when the landship suddenly stopped its forward motion with a jerk of hastily applied brakes.

⸺◦◯◦⸺

"Skipper, I swear that's a new mirror," Chief Scotty declaimed. "I inspected it thoroughly before we installed it at the Wichita terminal." He looked angry, and his eyes darted suspiciously from shadowed place to shadowed place as though looking for something hidden from casual view.

"He did, sir," Lieutenant Fletcher said. "I supervised him—and the crew—personally. The mirror was sound." He looked affronted.

"Then how did this happen?" Captain Pequod asked, glaring at the remains of the parabolic mirror, and the charred decking underneath it. He knew the damage could have been far worse; if the boiler room crew hadn't spotted the fire starting under the mirror so quickly, the entire landship could have gone up in flames.

"I intend to find out, sir," Fletcher said, drawing himself into a rigid position of attention.

"Aye, Skipper, we'll do just that," Scotty agreed.

Just as a sailing ship on the sea carried enough spare canvas and rope to replace all of its sails and lines if necessary, the *Argus* carried spare mirrors. In less than half an hour, a fresh parabolic mirror was in place, and steam was building again. The mighty landship began rolling once more.

Down below, in the undercarriage where there were no crewmen to see, and little light to see by if there had been, Spindlebrake chortled and dry-washed his hands as the brake cables snapped. He prepared to make the minute adjustments to the steering cables that would fine tune the direction in which the *Argus* was headed. High above, Malevolent Eye began lodging the blocks into the mirror mounts, rendering the mirrors immobile. Grimblelich was ready to relay steering instructions to Spindlebrake and kept watch for their unexpected destination. Unexpected, that is, by the humans on board.

Forward of the latticework tower holding the sunlight-focusing mirrors for the boiler stood a tall mast. The mast soared a hundred feet above the pilot house and was topped by a basket of a size and strength to hold two men; a crow's nest. The crow's nest was currently occupied by Ike Earp and Wyatt Clanton.

"Ah don' lak it," Ike Earp said, straining his voice to be heard above the wind that whistled past so high above the deck.

"Me neithuh," Wyatt Clanton agreed. "Tain't natural, th' problems they dun been havin' down inna boiler room."

Earp opened his mouth to make a further comment but had to grab tight onto the lip of the basket when the *Argus* unexpectedly lurched to the side. The wheels had hit a bump instead of being smoothly steered around it.

"Hey, who's steering down thar?!" Clanton yelled, his words whipping away before they reached the pilot house. He snarled something inarticulate at Earp, who suddenly grasped Clanton's arm tightly enough to affect the flow of blood.

"L-Look!" Earp mouthed, and let go of Clanton's arm with one hand to point at the horizon.

Clanton squinted into the distance, then hauled out his spyglass and held it to his eye. On the horizon, but approaching more rapidly than he was used to seeing things approach, was a hole in the prairie, about half a mile wide.

The *Argus* was heading straight for the hole.

Clanton dropped his spyglass and cranked the sound-powered phone. "We's off course and headin' straight fer a hole," he wheezed when the phone was answered.

Captain Pequod was on the bridge, shouting into speaking tubes. "What do you mean, you can't reduce power?" he demanded into one tube, speaking to Lieutenant Fletcher. Into another, he harangued Helmsman Crusher, "Steer, dammit, turn this ship!" But try as they might, Fletcher and Crusher could control neither the speed of the Argus, nor her vector. He looked out the forward windows. The great landship was now close enough to the massive crater that he could see it from his vantage point.

"It's gremlins I tell you!" Chief Scotty shouted.

"And I'm telling you there's no such thing as gremlins!" Lieutenant Fletcher shouted back.

Able-bodied landsman Sugarfoot wisely kept his peace and continued trying to adjust the final mirror reflecting onto the parabolic one that focused the sun's rays on the boiler.

Unseen or heard by the humans, Grimblelich crouched in his cubby, watching and listening, both hands clapped over his mouth to keep his laughs from escaping to where the humans could hear them.

"It's gremlins, and I'm a gonna find 'em!" Scotty roared. He hefted a huge pipe wrench and began stalking around the boiler room, peering into every shadow, poking the wrench into every cubby—except the one in which Grimblelich crouched.

Fletcher glowered at the chief boiler mate but didn't vocalize any of the swearing that he was doing on the inside. *Gremlins, indeed. Chief Scotty is around the bend and should be retired!*

Elsewhere, Helmsman Crusher abandoned his post to go below, into the bowels of the undercarriage, in search of what must be a jammed steering cable. What he found horrified him. As soon as he recovered enough of his wits, he found a sound-powered phone and signaled the bridge.

"Sir," he reported when he got Captain Pequod on the line, "every one of the brake cables is broken. I'm searching for a jam in the steering cables."

Pequod groaned. "First Officer Ishmael," he ordered, "assemble a work crew to repair the broken brake cables, if you please."

"Aye, aye, sir," Ishmael replied, and began snapping out orders to assemble the work party he'd need to perform the job. To himself, he wondered if there was enough time to repair a sufficient number of brake cables to stop the *Argus* before she dove into the crater. *Hmm, perhaps if we repair them on one side and applied only* those *brakes. That could slew the landship in that direction.*

⟶◦◗◖◦⟵

After breakfast, Cheyenne Walker went back to his cabin and into his trunk. A concealed compartment in the lid, when opened, revealed a knife with a ten-inch blade, a Bowie. He slid the knife into its scabbard and through the belt under his frock coat. It wasn't as well concealed as his Buntline Special, but he suspected the *Argus's* officers and crew would be too busy trying to bring the landship back under control to pay much attention to the passengers, as long as the passengers didn't get in their way. He rejoined Kitty Belle, who had, for propriety's sake, waited in the passageway outside his cabin, and they headed topside, to the mirrored latticework tower. As they had thought, the few officers and crewmen they encountered hurried from one place to another and paid them no mind. In minutes, they were at the base of the tower, looking for the threads their questing hands had found the previous night. They couldn't find them by eye, so they had to grope.

High above, Malevolent Eye kept fingers on each of the threads that linked the mirrors, and watched the two humans with intense curiosity, wondering what they were up to. He was certain that he wouldn't like it when he found out. He saw the larger of the two humans pull something out of his coat mere seconds after feeling a tremble in the threads. *A knife!*

Malevolent Eye let out a scream in such a high register that had there been any dogs on the Argus, it would have set them all to baying. As it was, every coyote within three miles howled at the sky.

He reached behind himself to the only missile he could bring to hand and flung it straight down at the human's knife hand.

"What the—!" Cheyenne Walker yelped when his hand was struck by a glob of smelly brown goop. He transferred his Bowie to his off hand and shook the goop away. He wiped the back of his hand against a piece of lattice as he looked upward to spy where the missile had come from. He looked just in time to dodge a second projectile, as equally stench-ridden as the first.

"There!" Kitty Belle shouted, looking at the top of the tower as she drew her Peacemaker. But before she could pull the trigger, something the size and shape of a tailless monkey without a bellhop cap, leapt and rammed into her arm, throwing her aim off and almost dislodging the pistol from her hand.

Walker grabbed for the gremlin, but it back-flipped away and his hand clutched air. Then he was yelping again and kicking one foot wildly—a third gremlin had latched onto his calf and was digging in with its talons.

Kitty Belle moved with more speed and strength than Walker would have credited her with; she grabbed his flailing foot with one hand and held it still for a precious second or two while she swung her Peacemaker, slamming it into the head of the beastie gouging Walker's leg. The gremlin flew off and thudded into a nearby bulkhead, where it lay unmoving.

Malevolent Eye continued pelting the humans with feces as he scrambled down the tower to join Grimblelich in his attack.

Kitty Belle did a better job of ignoring the bombardment than Cheyenne Walker did. Perhaps that was because Walker only had the one frock coat with him and didn't want it soiled.

They both took aim and fired at Grimblelich, but the gremlin was just as fast as Walker remembered, and all of their shots missed the darting, dashing gremlin as it closed on them. Grimblelich leapt at Walker. The man slashed with his Bowie knife, but met only air as the gremlin twisted out of the way and landed on the latticework instead. He immediately changed course and flew at Kitty Belle. She flung herself to the deck, letting the gremlin sail over her.

Malevolent Eye was now close enough to plunge off the tower, onto Walker's shoulders. He dug in with his claws and sank his teeth into the back of Walker's neck. The man screamed in pain and threw both hands back. Fortunately, Walker hadn't let go of either his pistol or knife, and both slammed into the gremlin. Malevolent Eye shrieked and let go, raking the top of Walker's shoulders as he dove away. Walker spun and flashed out with the knife, while bringing his Buntline Special to bear and pulled the trigger. The blade missed, but the bullet tore through the gremlin's upper arm, causing it to shriek out again, once more setting off all the coyotes within three miles.

Grimblelich, meanwhile, spun in midair so that he landed facing the woman who'd ducked beneath him. She was still down, facing away. He gave out a triumphant scream and dove at her, sinking his claws into her upward-jutting posterior. And shrieked in frustration when his claws met cloth, wire, and whalebone—he didn't know about bustles, and had always thought that human females were simply well endowed in the rear. He screamed even more frustration when he tried—and failed—to yank his claws out of the unexpected contraption. Two claws were stuck in whalebone struts, two others had gotten wire twisted around them, and another was entangled in a bow on the outside of the bustle.

Instantly realizing what must have happened, Kitty Belle rolled onto her back and slammed her buttocks onto the deck with all the force she could manage. Grimblelich went limp, stunned and with numerous broken bones. Kitty Belle struggled to her feet, not an easy task with the feebly moving gremlin attached to her bustle.

Malevolent Eye, despite his wounded arm, charged Walker again, and Spindlebrake had come to and was orienting himself on Kitty Belle. The two aimed and fired.

In the undercarriage, the work crew under the command of First Officer Ishmael, had reattached most of the cables on the port side brakes. Ishmael spoke into the sound-powered phone; "Sir, try the brakes. I think this will save us."

On the bridge, Captain Pequod gave the order. The port brakes bit, and the *Argus* slewed violently to the left, heeling almost far enough to capsize.

At the foot of the mirror tower, everyone was caught off guard. Cheyenne Walker and Kitty Belle tumbled, clutching at each other. Spindlebrake went head over heels and rolled off the deck to the desert floor. Malevolent Eye was in mid-leap, missing and slamming into the tower's base. Stunned, he simply slid along the canted deck until he followed Spindlebrake to the ground below.

Walker let go of Kitty Belle with one hand and gripped a door with the other. He hauled himself to his feet and helped her up. Somehow, she had managed to retain her grip on her Colt Peacemaker. Walker saw his Bowie knife lodged next to the crow's nest mast and shuffled to it. His Buntline Special was gone. He took the knife and slashed at the threads in the latticework tower. Abruptly, nearly invisible wedges fell from some of the mirror mounts, and the mirrors rotated so that most of the sun's light was no longer funneled down to the boiler room.

"Give me a hand here," Kitty Belle said.

Walker looked at where she plucked at the gremlin still attached to her bustle. He grinned as he stepped behind her to extract the beastie.

"Somebody had to have heard the gunfire," she said. "We better get below before anybody comes and finds us."

Walker nodded. "But I think we need to leave this where it'll be found, so the crew doesn't take the blame for this," he said, hefting the gremlin.

"Use your knife. Cut off one of the ribbons to tie it with," Kitty Belle said, pointing her bustle at him. She didn't object when his hands touched more of the area surrounding the bustle than was strictly necessary. As he dealt with the creature, she said all wide-eyed innocence, "You know, I was sent after a notorious gambler with a Bluntline Special... what a pity there's not one to be found on the *Argus*. I guess I'll have to keep looking."

Captain Pequod was grateful to whoever it was who left the bound gremlin on the deck where it was found after the *Argus* was stabilized. He knew that the broken creature would be all the proof he'd need at the court of inquiry convened to discover what had happened that nearly cost the Neo-Butterfield and Overland Line its flagship.

And not only did Cheyenne Walker go calling on Kitty Belle at the Oriental Hotel, he stayed for breakfast.

VEST OF THE PECOS

"MR. CHEYENNE WALKER, I DO DECLARE!"

The man in the vest slowly turned from the mirrored mast he leaned against watching the setting sun to look at the woman who spoke. He swept off his hat and bent in a courtly bow. "Miss Kitty Belle!"

"Why, so I am," said the green-eyed woman. Her ivory complexion and rosy lips were exactly as he remembered them.

When Cheyenne Walker first met Kitty Belle, she'd worn green sateen to match her eyes. This time her skirt's red evoked her lips. As on their first meeting, in deference to the heat, she wasn't wearing what must have been a matching jacket, and her blouse was unbuttoned just far enough to suggest the beginning of the valley between her breasts.

"Surely," Walker said, standing again, "Pinkerton isn't looking for me in Chihuahua."

"Indeed not," she said with a twinkle in her eyes. "The Agency is convinced that a certain gambling man is either dead in the wastes of Deseret, or has reached port in California and taken ship to the Antipodes."

He cocked his head and asked, "Did a report from a certain agent who had gone in search of the gambling man contribute to that supposition?"

She fluttered a fan in front of her face and allowed, "Perhaps." After a beat, during which he began to smile, she added, "Or perhaps not."

Before he could respond, a bell chimed from a nearby doorway. Instead of whatever he might have been about to say, he offered his arm and asked, "Shall we?" and cast a last glance at the mast, which he knew must focus sunlight to the below decks to make the steam that turned the river boat's paddle wheels.

"So gallant, Mr. Cheyenne Walker. Yes, we shall." She placed her hand on his forearm and they headed for the dining salon of the Rockies and Gulf, Ltd. paddle wheeler *Samuel Clemens* and the dinner that had been signaled by the chiming bell.

"What is that you're twirling in your fingers?" she asked as they strolled.

"What, this?" he replied, holding up for inspection a feather. "Just something I found on the deck."

"A raven's feather?"

It wasn't until later, over a postprandial cordial in the first-class salon, that Miss Kitty Belle, Pinkerton agent extraordinaire, told Mr. Cheyenne Walker how it happened that she was on the same paddle wheeler that he was on, heading down the Pecos River.

⟶◦◗◦◦⟵

"The Rockies and Gulf has employed the Agency to investigate the identity and method of a most extraordinary thief on their boats, including the *Samuel Clemens*," Kitty Belle said softly enough to not be overheard by others in the first-class salon.

Cheyenne Walker raised an eyebrow in question.

A slight smile danced lightly across her lips. "In the gambling salon," she amplified.

"Cheating at cards?" he asked, and slowly shook his head.

"Not card sharping," she said with a toss of her tresses, "nothing so simple or straight forward. The Rockies and Gulf believes they could easily enough find a card sharp and ban him from their ships—or turn him over to the next available sheriff. Rather, chips are taken from a winner as he is on his way to the cashier."

"A strongarm thief."

She waved a dismissive hand. "The winner leaves the table with a pocket or tray filled with chips, and the chips are mysteriously gone when he reaches the cashier's cage."

He gave her a skeptical look. "All of the gambler's chips are gone, and he didn't notice a thing?" He held up his hand before she could answer. "Chips? Before he's cashed them in? Don't you mean the thief takes the cash *after* the chips are cashed in?"

She smiled broadly. "As I said, this is a most extraordinary thief I seek. He takes only chips, never money."

"Strange, yes. But easy to solve when the thief attempts to cash in the chips without having won them."

Still smiling, she shook her head. "No one has attempted to cash in the chips."

Walker slowly shook his head. "I find that highly improbable."

She nodded. "So one might think. Some of the men who lost chips are well-known, powerful men. Some are physically powerful in their own right, and most are accompanied by bodyguards. A strongarm thief would not succeed any more than a card sharp would."

Walker cocked an eyebrow at that.

"Oh?" Kitty Belle cooed. "Are you saying they couldn't catch you?"

His eyes widened and he placed a hand over his heart. "I never said I cheated at cards—and no one has ever proved that I did!"

"So, it was merely a misunderstanding that sent me after you last year?" There was a twinkle in her eye as she said that.

Cheyenne Walker projected all innocence as he said nothing in response to the question. Instead, he asked, "What have you learned about the thief and his methods thus far?"

"Nothing. I am so far undercover on this mission that not even Captain P. H. Wilson knows my identity."

"I'm the only one aboard who knows you're—"

"Hush!" she said urgently and quietly. "That's right, you're the only one. Please don't expose me."

"No, ma'am. I am heartily sorry." His pained expression assured her that he truly was.

Her fingertips brushed the back of his hand where it rested on the arm of his chair. "Thank you." Recognizing that they had been looking conspiratous, she tossed her head and trilled a disarming laugh. "Laugh, you fool," she whispered from behind her fan. "Make them think we are exchanging risqué jokes, and not begin to think we're making nefarious plans."

Catching on to exactly what she meant, and recalling some of the glances that had been cast in their direction, he threw his head back and roared out a laugh. That drew more glances, but these were more disapproving than suspicious. Leaning close, he said behind a hand that hid his lips from prying eyes, "We aren't making *any* plans."

"But by *chance* we could be," she said, fluttering her eyelashes above her fan. She laughed loudly at his shocked expression.

More disapproving glances were cast their way.

Later, toward the witching hour, they left the first-class salon for the gambling salon.

Women weren't forbidden, per se, from entering the gambling salons on the steamships of Rockies and Gulf, Ltd.; but neither were they made to feel welcome—certainly not when unaccompanied, as Miss Kitty Belle would have been had it not been for the fortuitous appearance of Cheyenne Walker.

The men already there certainly noticed when Kitty Belle entered the salon on Walker's arm—she was, after all, the most beauteous woman on the *Samuel Clemens*. They eyed her—some surreptitiously, some openly, all speculatively, because they recognized that the two hadn't boarded together. The few other women who were in the gambling salon looked at her quite differently from how the men did—also because they knew that Kitty Belle and Cheyenne Walker hadn't arrived together; they disapproved of her.

Kitty Belle ignored the sniffs of the other women. Cheyenne Walker walked with more of a strut for the benefit of the other men; he was, after all, the man with the most desirable woman on his arm.

Cheyenne Walker was a gambling man; he made his way in the world by besting other men at games of chance, mostly cards. By his reckoning, winning at cards wasn't a matter of chance, but rather one of skill. And he was very skilled. So much so that he was more than once accused of cheating. But no one could ever prove that he marked cards—and nobody ever called him Ace-Up-His-Sleeve Walker.

The salon had a wheel of fortune, a roulette table, and five card tables with little maneuvering space between them. Gamblers at four of the tables played poker; the fifth was for Blackjack. No cash or gold dust was in evidence; shiny chips in a rainbow of colors were stacked in front of the players. A copper-faced man wearing a reservation hat with an eagle feather stuck in its band sat cross-legged on the floor near the entrance door. Walker was surprised that an Indian was allowed in the gambling salon but paid the man no further attention. A wrought-iron cashier's cage occupied the corner farthest from the salon's entrance. Three men, all armed, resided in the cage with the cashier. Two stewards moved about, serving drinks and adjusting the oil lamps as needed. There were windows, all closed against bats and nocturnally flying insects.

Walker was welcomed at a table; Miss Kitty Belle's presence at his shoulder virtually guaranteed his welcome somewhere—even if the female companions of the other players at the table would have preferred otherwise.

Duke Grangerford, Jim Douglas, Sid Thatcher, and Tom Lumberman were the men already seated at the table. Joanna, Sid's wife, sharply pinched her husband's earlobe when she saw him smile at Kitty Belle. Jim's wife, Sally, dug her fingernails into his neck at the edge of his collar for the same offense. Neither Duke Grangerford nor Tom Lumberman were accompanied. Kitty Belle hid her amusement behind her fan. Walker hadn't noticed the wives' reactions; when he sat to cards, he was at work. He paid attention to the men, deciding from whom he would win the most, and who he would strive to avoid bankrupting.

Sid Thatcher was returning home to El Paso after having constructed a hotel in Denver. Jim Douglas and his bride were on their honeymoon, thinking that a riverboat ride on the wild Pecos was all the adventure they could want before settling down to their anticipated life of married bliss. Tom Lumberman had made a minor gold strike in the Sangre de Christos and was returning east before the gold bug got too deep a bite on him.

Duke Grangerford, though, with his generous paunch, looked like an overly-prosperous banker. The kind who foreclosed on farms and turned around to sell the land to cattle barons at a huge profit—exactly the kind of man Walker delighted in besting at cards.

Grangerford was also the one to whom Kitty Belle paid the most attention; especially after she noticed the two toughs who sat quietly near the salon's windows. The looks they occasionally exchanged with Grangerford made it abundantly clear that they were his bodyguards. He, she was certain, was most likely the next victim of the mysterious thief.

They played for the best part of an hour, with Walker winning small amounts from Jim and Tom, somewhat more from Sid, and yet more from Duke. But not too much; the trip down the Pecos would take several days, and he didn't want to win too much too soon, thinking it better to take time building his stake.

"Gentlemen, this has been a refreshing game, giving a sporting rise to the blood," Grangerford said as he pushed away from the table. The two toughs moved instantly to his side, helping him to his feet. "But the growling of my stomach tells me I must have a snack, and then retire to my bed. I shall be most happy to rejoin you on tomorrow's eve to reacquire the monies you won from me this evening." He gave a curt bow and turned toward the cashier's cage. One of the toughs scooped Duke's chips into a chip tray and carried it in the banker's wake.

Before the trio reached the cashier's cage, there was a clattering of thrown latches and all of the salon's windows flew open to let a mighty gust of wind blow through, extinguishing all the lights.

"Nobody move!" one of the stewards shouted loud enough to be heard over the chorus of voices exclaiming in surprise at the sudden lack of illumination.

"We'll have the lights back in a moment!" shouted the other just as loudly.

True to their word, both men quickly had Lucifers struck and went about the salon reigniting the wicks of the oil lamps. Everyone was still where they'd been when the room went dark, except Cheyenne Walker and Kitty Belle, who had both risen the instant the windows flew open and began moving toward Duke Grangerford and his toughs. They stopped, almost at the trio who were advancing to the cashier's cage, and took in the room's tableau.

"Is this what happens?" Walker asked.

"Not that I have previously heard," Kitty Belle answered.

Several people, including the toughs and one of the armed guards in the cage, looked at them suspiciously. In barely two more steps, Duke Grangerford reached his destination and half-turned to the tough carrying his chip tray.

"Where are they?" Grangerford shouted, feeling the unexpected lightness of the tray. He looked into it and yelped in outrage—it was empty. The chips were gone.

Red in the face, he turned the rest of the way and screamed at the unfortunate tough, "What did you do with my chips?" Spittle flew from his lips, stippling the retainer's face.

"What?" the tough exclaimed, shocked at the accusation. "N-n-nothing! They were here! I-I didn't do anything with your chips except hand you the tray!"

"Did the chips fall out onto the floor then?" Grangerford made an exaggerated show of examining the floor in search of his missing chips. "No! They aren't on the floor, are they? You had them, they must be in your pockets!" He lunged at the tough's pants pockets, only to have his hands slapped away.

"You hired me to guard you," the tough snarled. "Laying hands on my person is not part of our arrangement!"

Grangerford backed off and gaped at the tough, shocked at being so spoken to by an underling. He spun to the cashier's cage and pointed at the armed guards, "I demand that you place this miscreant under arrest!"

The three guards exchanged quick glances, then looked at the cashier for guidance.

The cashier looked like he wanted nothing to do with these matters, but only for a second or two. Then he bucked up and said firmly, "I'm sorry, sir, but the guards only have jurisdiction over the cage and what is inside it. If your chips are missing, that is your responsibility."

Grangerford grew redder in the face and filled his chest to roar out at the cashier but stopped when another voice interrupted him.

"Sir, I believe your man is innocent of stealing your chips."

Everybody turned to the speaker, a non-descript individual who had been dallying about the roulette table without putting a chip on a number.

Grangerford, having been deflected from attacking his bodyguard, still felt the need to shout out his displeasure, so shout he did. "And just who are you?"

"I, sir," the man said, standing and taking a knee in a sarcastic manner, "am Driscoll Chambers."

"Well, *tra-la-la*. So, who do you think is guilty, then?"

He swept his arm out to point in an accusatory manner. "No one but the two who are not still in the places they occupied before the lights went out!"

"Yes, it must be them!" someone agreed. "I saw them whispering in a most suspicious manner earlier in the first-class salon."

"As did I," another chimed in.

"I knew they were up to no good!" Joanna Thatcher cried. "You should have seen them in the first-class salon, they looked more guilty than an honest person could conceive!"

"Take them!" Grangerford ordered.

"Be still!" Kitty Belle snapped at Walker as one of the toughs spun her about and grasped her arms from behind, securing them in a steely grip.

The tough who'd been accused shipped out his pistol and aimed it at the center of Walker's face. "Move and I'll kill you," he said, smiling now that he was no longer the object of accusation.

Walker slowly moved his hands from near his sides and held them with palms forward and fingers spread.

The cashier blew into the speaking tube to the pilot house. "Sir," he said when the first officer answered, "we have just had an attempted theft. The miscreants, a man and a woman, have been apprehended. What are your orders?" He listened for a moment, then said, "No, sir. It was a gentleman on the floor who apprehended them. The cage guards are still at their station." Again, he listened, then said, "I will indeed, sir, thank you, sir." He turned to the cage guards. "Bosun Dawson is on his way to take custody of the prisoners. Until he gets here, draw your weapons and aim them at the thieves. If either of them attempts to escape, shoot them both."

"Now see here—" Walker began, but shut up and raised his hands to shoulder level when the bodyguard holding his pistol on him twitched his weapon's muzzle.

The minutes seemed to drag into near eternity while they waited for the bosun but were actually no more than three or four; having pistols pointed at one's person can distort time terribly.

"What have we here?" a powerful voice boomed.

All heads turned toward the entrance to the gambling salon, where stood a veritable mountain of a man, flanked by two strapping young men, each bigger than he was. Bosun Dawson quickly took in the scene and ordered his two mates, "Secure him," meaning Cheyenne Walker. To Kitty Belle he said, "Ma'am, if you give me your bond, I will not have you in chains, but will allow you the freedom to walk on your own to the brig."

"I do, sir," she replied with a nod of her head and as much dignity as she could manage with her arms pinioned behind her back.

The man with the eagle feather in his reservation hat silently and without expression, watched the proceedings.

It was morning, past the breakfast hour, by the time Captain P. H. Wilson paid a visit to the storeroom where Miss Kitty Belle and Cheyenne Walker, with his hands no longer bound, were incarcerated. They both rose at his entrance. The captain stood, studying them wordlessly for long moments before speaking.

"I am hard pressed to believe that you are the thieves," he began. "Last night was not the first time such a theft happened on my riverboat. Neither of you was with me when it happened before. That tells me that unless you are members of a criminal enterprise whose members all conduct their operations in exactly the same manner, you are innocent of this theft. More, my bosun carefully searched the gambling salon, and both of your cabins, even though there was no way you could have spirited the chips there during the brief time the lamps were extinguished." He made a face. "He did, however, make an interesting discovery among each of your belongings.

"Yet everybody who saw you in the first-class salon agrees that you were talking in a most conspiratory manner," he went on before either could ask about the 'interesting discoveries,' though they both knew what he must have meant. "Further, you didn't board the *Samuel Clemens* together. You, sir, boarded in Espanola, but you, miss, didn't board until Pueblo Las Vegas. How do you explain yourselves?"

Kitty Belle made a moue. "That question, sir, would have been answered last night had anybody conducted a search of my purse. Sheer carelessness." Not only had her purse not been searched, nobody had taken it away from her. She opened it and withdrew a leather wallet which she handed to the captain.

He opened it and stared at what it held for a long moment before raising his gaze to her and asking with surprise, "*You're* a Pinkerton agent?"

"I am."

"That explains the Colt Peacemaker hidden in your luggage." His eyes suddenly grew wide in offended shock. "Then you must be on my boat because of…" His voice trailed off and he looked inward.

She said, "I am in possession of a letter assigning me to investigate the series of mysterious thefts aboard the Pecos River riverboats of the Rockies and Gulf Line. Your bosun must have missed it when he searched my cabin."

Wilson's visage grew dark at the explanation. "No one saw fit to tell me of a criminal investigation being conducted on my very own boat. Do they think I'm involved?" he demanded with fury in his voice.

"I'm sure nobody suspects you, captain," she said quickly. "The thinking was more likely that if you knew, then someone else who might be involved could possibly gain the same information, and my presence would be for naught."

Wilson snorted, obviously disbelieving the explanation, but willing to accept it for the moment. Instead, he said, "And no one examined your persons or property seeking the missing chips?"

"That's right," Walker said, shaking his head.

"I would have kicked anyone who attempted to search me," Kitty Belle said, and turned an ankle to show the captain how firm and pointed the toes of her shoes were.

"I know who the lady is," Wilson said, turning to Walker, "but who are you, sir? Do you also have Pinkerton credentials? You have the look of a gambling man."

"No, captain. I'm a private citizen, not a Pinkerton. Miss Belle and I are old acquaintances, and it is coincidence we're on the same riverboat." He shrugged at the unlikeliness of it.

Wilson grunted. "What about the other part of my question, are you a gambling man?"

"I am. But I play at cards and win through skill, not artifice. You can see I'm not wearing a frock coat, just shirt sleeves, as I was last night in the gambling salon. No traps, no hidden cards, not even a ring," he displayed his fingers, "with a hidden blade to mark cards."

"How do you explain your conspiratorial whisperings?"

"Captain," Kitty Belle said, a small smile on her lips, "As Mister Walker said, we have a lengthy acquaintanceship. We were discussing pleasurable events we have shared, and interesting people we have met on our occasional traveling encounters."

Wilson looked for a crate or chest to sit on, decided on one, brushing off a paw print, and lowered himself onto it. "Please," he said, gesturing for them to also sit. The captain lost himself in thought for a few moments before asking, "Everybody, or nearly everybody, thinks we caught the thief. So, what am I to do with you? I can't hold a Pinkerton agent under lock and key, certainly not one operating on instructions from my employer." He looked at Walker. "You, on the other hand, I can hold as a possible risk to other gamers."

Kitty Belle put her hand on Walker's arm to prevent him from speaking without thought. "Captain, please don't do that," she said. "I had a difficult case a year ago on which Mr. Walker was of inestimable assistance. The more I learn about the thefts on your riverboat, the more I suspect I will need his aid to resolve this case."

"Do you have any idea of who is doing the thefts, or how they are doing it?" When she didn't answer, the captain looked at Walker and asked, "Either of you?"

Before the silence grew too lengthy, there was a light tapping at the door.

Wilson glanced at the two, then at the door. He stood to open it.

The man who'd sat cross-legged in the gambling salon the night before stood before him, his reservation hat with its eagle feather in his hands.

"I know who you are," the Indian said, addressing Kitty Belle, "and you as well," to Cheyenne Walker. Back to Kitty Belle, "I also know why you are here, and I can answer questions for you. May I?" The last two words were to Captain Wilson, who stepped aside so the Indian could enter the storeroom. As the night before, he sat cross-legged on the floor rather than sitting on a crate as did everybody else.

"You know who we are," Wilson said. "Who are you?"

"Most whites call me Joe," the Indian answered calmly.

"Injun Joe. Right," Captain P. H. Wilson said with a snort.

The Indian ignored the captain's remark. "You seek to stop the stealing of the gambling chips," he said to Kitty Belle, with an including nod to Cheyenne Walker, "and to solve the mystery of the darkening of light that happens before the thefts."

She nodded. "That's true. What do you know about it?"

"It is the Trickster, and—"

"The Trickster!" Wilson yelped, interrupting the Indian. "That's Coyote, it's only an Indian superstition. Coyote doesn't exist!"

"Do you have a better explanation, captain?" Joe asked calmly. Wilson sputtered.

"But Coyote plays tricks," Walker said slowly. "He's not a thief."

"Exactly," Kitty Belle agreed. "Why would Coyote steal the chips? And even if he is the thief, why doesn't he wait until the chips are cashed in so he can take the money?"

Joe nodded. "Coyote tricks. Darkening the lights is a trick. It is Raven who steals."

"But why steal gambling chips? Why not money?" Walker asked.

"He's looking for something?" Joe shrugged.

"Coyote *and*...?" Wilson yelled. "You expect me to believe *two* superstitions? Get off my boat!"

Joe the Indian stood, looking calmly at Kitty Belle the entire time. "Think about the chips, why Coyote and Raven would want things that are of no use to them," he said. "You have all you need to solve the mystery and stop the thefts." With a nod to Walker, he left the storeroom. Nobody saw Injun Joe again before the *Samuel Clemens* docked in Brownsville, Republic of Tejas.

Captain P. H. Wilson alternately roared and muttered after Joe departed. All that came through clearly was, "...stupid Injun superstitions..." "...gamblers who claim they don't cheat..." and "...women Pinkerton agents, what's the world coming to?" At length he calmed down, though his face was still red, and he still blew hard, like a snorting bull.

"I have no grounds to hold you," he said, "or to restrict you to your cabins. Nor even to hold your weapons." He went away inside his mind for a moment, picturing the cabin plan and where the two were billeted relative to each other. Not close enough to conspire.

"You," he said to Walker, "are released to do what you wish, including playing at cards. With conditions. You will wear neither frock coat nor rings in the gambling salon, and you will turn your shirtsleeves up when you are at play. I want no one to have suspicion that you are cheating.

"And you, miss, will not stand at any table at which Mr. Walker is playing. This is to alleviate any suspicion that you are signaling him as to the cards in other players' hands.

"Furthermore, should the lights unexpectedly extinguish, you will remain in place until the stewards restore illumination. Do you understand?"

"I do, captain," Walker said. "Except I enjoy having Miss Kitty Belle standing by my side. But—" He held up his hand and raised his voice to continue talking over Wilson's interruption, "—I understand your concern and will forgo the pleasure of her nearness."

The captain grunted and looked at the Pinkerton agent.

She nodded, with a slight smile on her lips. "That affords me better license to observe what is happening, which increases my chances of making a discovery. I readily comply, captain."

Somewhat mollified, Wilson's breath slowed and the color of his face began returning to normal. "As long as we are understood." He fished his watch out of his waistcoat pocket and popped its lid. "Early luncheon will be served shortly for the late risers. I suggest you avail yourselves of it. I will instruct the bosun to return your weapons to your cabins." He snapped his watch closed, stood, and exited the storeroom.

"Now what?" Walker asked Kitty Belle. His eyes followed the captain, relieved that he hadn't had to explain how he happened to have a Buntline Special in his luggage.

"I am going to retire to my cabin and refresh myself." She briefly sniffed. "I suggest you do the same." Without another glance at him, she left. He momentarily followed, heading to his own cabin to clean himself.

Captain Wilson didn't believe the Indian. He thought that Coyote and Raven were nonsense. Both Cheyenne Walker and Kitty Belle, however, had spent much time on the ground in the West, not only on the rivers as the captain had. They had both seen things that were unknown to the denizens of more civilized climes. They were not about to discount what Joe had told them, no matter how unreal it sounded. The last thing the Indian had told them was to look at the chips. What was special about the chips, they wondered, that would entice Raven to steal them? And why would Coyote help

Raven? Their discussion over the early luncheon that was set out for late risers reached no conclusions. Nor did their further discussions as they walked the promenade afterward, nor their conversation at the evening's dinner. After dining, they decided to retire to their respective cabins and rest until after dark, at which time they would return to the gaming salon, him to play, her to detect.

After the previous night's accusation, most players were reluctant to allow Cheyenne Walker to join their table. Four of the players even left the salon when he asked to sit in on their games. Some players shuffled about until they were all at tables that had no remaining open seats for him. He didn't let it bother him. Instead, he got some chips and a deck of cards, sat at an empty table and began playing solitaire—against himself, for money. After half an hour he noticed how shiny the chips were, and recalled that Ravens were attracted to small shiny things. Could that be it, could Raven take the chips because they were shiny?

But why would Coyote help Raven? He couldn't suss that.

As on the previous night, the salon's windows were closed—but not shuttered. He stood and stepped to the nearest window. He unlatched and raised the sash and peered out to both sides and above, but didn't see a person, much less an Indian demi-god.

"Coyote," he said softly, "You must be out there. It's time you and Raven stopped frightening people."

"I'm sorry, sir," a voice said next to Walker's shoulder, "but the windows must remain closed." The speaker, one of the stewards, reached past Walker to lower the sash. He did it fast enough that Walker had to yank his hands back so they wouldn't be smashed between sash and sill.

"Sorry. I didn't know." Walker stepped away from the window and resumed his seat. During the short time he'd been at the window, two men had entered the room and sat at his table. One of them was Driscoll Chambers, the man who the previous night had accused Cheyenne Walker and Kitty Belle of stealing Grangerford's chips. Walker gave him a level look and waited for him to say something.

Chambers gave him a crooked grin and said with a shrug, "Who else could it have been? You were the only ones who had moved. Everyone else was still in place when the stewards relit the lamps."

Walker grunted, and looked at the other man—the tough who had carried Grangerford's tray of chips.

"No one speaks to me the way that rich bastard did," the tough snarled. "He did, so I quit!"

"What's your name, friend?" Chambers asked, extending his hand to shake.

"Angelo." The tough shook Chambers' hand, looked to see if Walker would shake with him. Walker did, but pointedly did not offer his hand to Chambers.

"Cut for the deal?" Walker asked, putting the cards down in the middle of the table.

Angelo turned over the nine of clubs, Chambers' was the six of diamonds. Walker turned up the jack of hearts.

"Dealers choice?" he asked. The others nodded. "Five card stud."

Over the next hour, four other men entered the gambling salon, three of whom joined Walker's table. He soon enough had a respectable pile of chips in front of him. A casual look around the salon told him that nobody else was much of a winner on this night, that if anyone was going to tempt Coyote and Raven it would have to be him.

He yawned widely and said, "Gents, I had a trying time last night and sleep beckons. I'll give you another chance tomorrow."

There were general murmurs of disappointment from the others at not having more opportunity to recoup their losses from him, but all agreed that they'd win from him the next night. Walker scooped his chips into a tray, stood, and headed for the cashier's cage. He walked closer to the windows than he really needed to and held the tray one-handed so that its contents were clearly visible to any secret watchers without.

There was a jangle as the latches on all the windows were thrown and bangs as the sashes flew up. Wind blustered through the suddenly open windows, blowing out the flames in the oil lamps, casting the salon into darkness.

Walker was expecting the wind and the dark. The instant he felt a buffet he slapped out with his free hand and his fingers grasped empty air.

"Remain calm!" the stewards shouted. "Stay where you are! We will restore the light quickly!"

Lucifers were struck, and lamps resumed burning as the stewards bustled about lighting them.

Walker looked at his hands. All they held was an empty tray. But he thought his hand had brushed feathers.

"Raven!" he whispered.

"Superstition about an Indian demi-god or not, captain," Miss Kitty Belle said a short time later in the dining salon, "we are now certain of the involvement of a raven in the thefts." She, Cheyenne Walker, Bosun Dawson, and Captain Wilson were seated at the Captain's table—the only people in the room save for a single steward woken to serve late-night coffee and cakes. "And that," she pointed at a spot on the rug, "looks suspiciously like a coyote's print. It's not the first I've seen on this voyage. And both Mister Walker and I have seen raven's feathers. Have other passengers seen such?"

"But how could...?" Wilson's voice trailed off; he was unwilling to give voice to what everybody, including him, was thinking.

"An ordinary raven couldn't have taken the chips from the tray," Miss Kitty Belle said, sure of what the captain hadn't been able to say.

"An ordinary raven would have knocked the tray out of my hands," Walker amplified.

Dawson snorted. "If'n the dumb bird didn't first knock itself out on sumpin else getting to the tray."

"Have others seen such things?" Walker demanded, unwilling to let the question about other passengers go unanswered.

Reluctantly, Captain Wilson nodded.

The boson grimaced. "I've seen a plenty o'em around the 'No Admittance' hatch t' the below decks."

"So, what are we going to do?" Kitty Belle asked. She was looking at Wilson, but the question was directed at Walker.

He thought for a long moment, then addressed the bosun. "Do you have any nets?"

"Cargo nets. But they're too big mesh to catch a bird."

"But not too big to catch a coyote?"

Dawson gave a snaggletoothed grin and nodded. "My nets kin do that."

Captain Wilson groaned; even his bosun was falling prey to the superstitions about Indian demi-gods.

"Fishing line," Kitty Belle suddenly said. "You do have fishing line, don't you?"

"Yes a'um, shore do. Lots a fishing line. Even got sailors good at macrame."

"And knot tying?" Walker asked, having immediately guessed what Kitty Belle had in mind.

"They're sailors, so they're real good at tying knots." Dawson's grin spread across his face.

Kitty Belle looked around to make sure all the windows were tightly closed, then leaning over the table, gestured for the others to come in close.

"Here's what we're going to do..." she said barely above a whisper.

"I wish to see the below decks," Walker said when she was through.

"Why on earth do you want to see the below decks?" Wilson asked.

"I'll never know until I look."

"Show him the way," the captain said to the bosun.

There were paw prints not only on the flooring outside the 'No Admittance' hatch, but on the steep stairs leading to the boat's bowels, as though a big dog had leapt down them.

The engineer's mate stood at the foot of the stairs, massive arms folded over his equally over-large chest.

"You Walker?" the mate asked.

"I am he, indeed."

"Bosun tol' me t' show you aroun'."

"Lead on, sir."

"Ain't no 'sir.' I'm a mate, I werks fer a livin'."

"No offense meant, mate. I can see you're a working man."

The below decks were dimly lit by oil lamps, and deep shadows lurked in odd places, as well as in all the expected locations. The mate picked up a hurricane lamp and adjusted its wick to cast the best light. As Walker had expected, two mirrored masts, one of which he had leaned against, penetrated from above, focusing their light during the day on the bottom of a huge boiler. A jigsaw of pipes led out of its top to a complex tangle of gears and axels, which eventually reached the turning gears for the great wheels that, one on each side, propelled the river boat. Pipes led back from the beginning of the jigsaw to the bottom of the boiler. Another pipe ran from one side of the below decks into the boiler.

"Thit brings water fum the river t' top off the boiler," the mate explained.

Walker nodded knowingly, although he really didn't understand the workings of a solar boiler.

"Do you have a dog down here?" he asked.

"Nope. Ain't no ani-mutts 'llowed in the below decks," the mate said, offended.

"I only ask because those look like the prints of a very big dog."

The mate looked where Walker pointed. "Ain't seen no dog," he said. "Ain't heared one, neither."

Walker looked into nowhere in particular, considering, then asked, "Have you seen any sign of a raven?"

"A raven? Ain't thit a bird?"

"A big bird."

"Got feathers like this?" The mate led the way to a scarred desk and picked a black feather off it.

"Exactly like that."

"Whadayano. Thot when I was at mess sumone put this here to jape on me. Ya thinks a bird been down here?"

Walker shrugged, and looked around some more. The mate had shown him everyplace except...

Walker picked up a hammer from a tool chest next to the desk and walked to the boiler.

"What's inside here?" he asked.

"Jist water turnin' to steam."

Walker looked speculatively at the boiler, then gave it a sharp rap with the hammer.

"Hey, don' do thit! You could bust a seam."

"Maybe, maybe not." He tapped the boiler again, less sharply this time. "You hear that?"

"Do thit agin," the mate said, leaning toward the boiler, looking confused.

Walker tapped the boiler again.

"Sumpin's in there ain't supposed t' be."

Walker asked Captain P. H. Wilson and the engineer to join him and the mate in the below decks, where he repeated his hammer experiment.

"What do you think that might be?" the engineer asked. He made himself busy helping the mate to drain and open the boiler.

Walker swore all of them to secrecy.

Two mornings later, going around the Big Bend of the Rio Grande River, they were ready.

"This isn't going to accomplish anything," Captain P. H. Wilson declared, looking at the preparations that had been made in the gambling salon of the *Samuel Clemens*.

"That remains to be seen, cCaptain," Miss Kitty Belle replied. Her eyes glistened, and the tip of her tongue briefly flickered across her lower lip. "That remains to be seen."

Bosun Dawson's chest puffed out with pride; he was confident that what he and his crew had assembled would accomplish the intended job, no matter what the captain thought. His chest deflated and he said morosely, "The thefts only happen once a trip. Why do you think we'll get another one this trip?"

"As you said, only once on a voyage," Kitty Belle said. "But the thief has already struck twice, so why not a third time?"

"The Trickster does what you don't expect," Cheyenne Walker added.

Kitty Belle nodded pleased agreement at him. "Gentlemen, if you would be so good," she said to the two stewards, in attendance at an earlier than usual hour for them. They began moving around the room, serving drinks to imaginary players. At a signal from the Pinkerton agent, two bosuns mates rattled latches. The stewards flinched, but managed to drop their serving trays and grab concealed cords without delay.

They did it three more times, each time faster and more smoothly than the time before.

When the stewards were dismissed and the door closed behind them, Bosun Dawson put his mates through their drill. They were much sharper than the stewards had been and mastered their chores in two tries. Still, the bosun put them through the drill twice more.

At last Kitty Belle said, "I do believe we are as ready as we can be. It is, I am sure, nearly past time for luncheon, so I suggest we retire to the dining salon for a midday repast." She looked brightly at Captain Wilson, who returned a curt nod.

"Are you ready?" she asked Cheyenne Walker.

He smiled, nodded slowly, and patted his trouser pocket.

Captain Wilson shook his head, he didn't like any of this, but he was desperate to put an end to the thefts.

She and Walker retired to their cabins for a rest before what they anticipated would be a long night.

There was general grumbling from the men who were denied entry to the gambling salon until well past dark; a few, mostly in the person of Duke Grangerford, objected quite loudly. He was grudgingly mollified when Captain P. H. Wilson promised him an extra stack of chips, courtesy of the Rockies and Gulf, for the inconvenience. Grangerford retired with poor grace to the dining salon to drink until summoned to the card tables.

It was past ten in the evening when Miss Kitty Belle, on Cheyenne Walker's arm, reappeared at the closed door of the gambling salon. Captain Wilson arrived at the same time, escorting Duke Grangerford. They all stepped aside to allow the cashier and his three armed guards passage; the guards carried the locked chests that held the night's supply of chips. Wilson unlocked the door and closed it again once the four had gone through. A moment later, the cashier called out all secure, and the captain opened the door to let the gamblers in. Anxious to begin playing at cards, none of them remarked on the presence of Bosun Dawson and the bosun's mates who stood spaced about the room. Nor did any of them take any particular note of the knotty decorations that hadn't been present on previous nights.

On this night, Cheyenne Walker played more seriously than he had previously on the *Samuel Clemens*. The pile of chips in front of him grew, at first slowly, then faster. But not so fast as to clean out the other players at his table, although some decided to attempt to change their luck by joining other games. They were always quickly replaced by others wishing to turn the cards.

Kitty Belle moved about the room, now stopping at this table, now at that, but never at Cheyenne Walker's table, in accordance with Captain Wilson's stricture.

Duke Grangerford glowered mightily as his pile of chips steadily shrank through the night. He couldn't help but see that most of them were going to Walker. He watched carefully, unable to see how the man cheated. Not only was Walker not wearing a frock coat, he even had his shirt sleeves turned up almost to his elbows—It wasn't possible for him to be slipping hidden cards. Not unless—

"Stop!" Grangerford shouted when Walker stretched and linked his hands behind his head. "Don't move!" He rose to his feet, and a derringer shot from his sleeve to his hand, pointed at Walker. "You're cheating, you must be!" He gestured to his sole remaining bodyguard. "His collar, he must have cards hidden in the back of his waistcoat! Search him."

Walker, normally slow moving, sprang to the side, crashing into Sid Thatcher, who was sitting next to him, and tumbling him to the floor. Thatcher's legs hit the table hard as he went over, spilling piles of chips and scattering some on the floor.

Grangerford reflexively pulled the trigger of his derringer at Walker's sudden move. His shot went wild, shattering a window. There was sudden silence, not even the *snick* of a dealt card hitting a tabletop. Everyone turned to the report of the derringer.

Fumbling, Grangerford broke his miniature firearm open and ejected the brass, but before he could jam another round into it Bosun Dawson wrapped his arms around him from behind, lifted him off his feet, and slammed him to the floor, straddling his chest and pinning his arms down with his knees.

"Bu-bu-but—" Grangerford sputtered. "Let me up! He's cheating!"

Walker, meanwhile, had gained his feet and faced the bodyguard.

The bodyguard hadn't moved toward him, but stood with his hands open and raised to chest level, showing that he wasn't armed. "I got no quarrel with you, Mr. Walker." He turned his face to Grangerford and said, "I was watching him, Mr. Grangerford. He weren't cheating."

"Yo-yo-you, you're fired!" Grangerford shrilled as best he could while pinioned to the floor.

"You can't fire me. I quit." He nodded at Walker, and started to leave the gambling salon but back-pedaled rapidly when Captain Wilson stormed into the salon, pushing back the gamblers and their women who'd suddenly decided on the better part of valor and were headed for the exit.

"What's going on here?" Wilson roared. "Who discharged a pistol on my boat?" His eyes first lit on Walker, then he noticed Grangerford struggling under Dawson.

"He made an accusation of cheating," Dawson said, giving the banker's chest a shove to keep him down. "He fired a derringer. It's there." He nodded at where the single-shot pistol lay on the floor a couple of feet from Grangerford's hand.

"Let him up!" Wilson snapped.

Dawson looked at his captain for a moment, then pushed down hard on Grangerford and lunged off him to snatch up the derringer before the banker could twist around to grab it. On his feet, he shoved the small pistol into his hip pocket.

Nobody moved to help Grangerford as he struggled, panting, to stand. "He-he," he thrust an accusing hand at Walker, "he cheated! I don't know how, but nobody can win as steady as he did unless he cheats!"

"Captain," Walker said, "I don't cheat. He said I have cards in the back of my vest." He took it off and turned around to show that he didn't have anything on his back, handed the vest to Wilson to check it for hiding places. "Do you want to examine my shirt?" he asked when the captain returned the vest.

Wilson glared at him for a moment, then turned his glare on Grangerford before facing Walker again. "That won't be necessary. Cash in your chips. You are hereafter banned from the gambling salon. And I would appreciate it if you confined yourself to your cabin except for meals and calls of nature."

Walker gave him a steady look before nodding curtly. After putting his vest back on and buttoning it, he stepped to the table and scooped all the chips at his place into a tray. It was the largest collection of chips anyone had amassed on the trip down the Pecos and Rio Grande Rivers. He went closer to the right side of the room than the center, with the tray in his right hand, and his left in his trouser pocket.

"Everybody ready?" he asked, to the confusion of all except the stewards, the bosun's mates, Kitty Belle, and Captain Wilson.

The rattle of latches being thrown sounded in the salon. The stewards had put down their drink trays and were taking hold of the concealed cords when Walker spoke. They yanked and the lamps were doused before the windows flew open and the wind swirled in.

"Heave!" Bosun Dawson bellowed. "Ho!" cried the mates. There was sudden clatter of chips and chip tray hitting the floor, the howl of a coyote, a rustling of wings, and the outraged caws of a bird.

"Lights!" Walker shouted.

The stewards scurried about, using Lucifers to relight the lamps. Gasps were emitted by the assembled people at the strange and totally unexpected sight that met their eyes—unexpected by all except Cheyenne Walker and Kitty Belle.

A coyote the size of a brown bear stood well-balanced on top of the nets intended to capture him with his mouth open in laughter, and a raven of size to rival the biggest eagle anyone present had ever seen perched on the sill of a window that had recently been securely closed.

"Coyote and Raven, I do believe," Kitty Belle said, nodding at the demi-gods. "Trickster and thief together. My, my..."

The gigantic coyote huffed, and growled deep in his chest; the growl sounded strangely human. He glared at Grangerford. The huge raven's red eyes darted from Walker to Kitty Belle to Grangerford; had its caw been human words it sounded like a promise to peck out the banker's eyes and rip open his guts to devour his liver.

Walker simply looked at them calmly. Kitty Belle laughed a tinkling merriment.

Coyote then spoke in human words, which were difficult but not impossible to understand. "You know why we are here," he said looking back and forth between Cheyenne Walker and Miss Kitty Belle.

"We do," Walker said at the same time as Miss Kitty Belle. He drew out the object he'd been clutching in his pocket, an oilskin-wrapped package and unwrapped it, displaying a decorated leather bag and an opened envelope.

"I believe this belongs to Raven," Walker said, holding out the bag.

The Raven cawed and swooped through the room to snatch it from his hand. In a trice, the two demi-gods were gone.

""And this," Walker said, handing the envelope to Miss Kitty Belle, "is the evidence you need to place Duke Grangerford into custody."

She accepted the envelope, examined it contents, and said to Captain Wilson, "Sir, if you will read these, I believe you will assist me by placing Mister Grangerford in shackles."

Wilson read the documents proffered, raised his eyebrows, and said to Bosun Dawson, "Lock him away."

"Gladly, sir."

"But, but—" Grangerford objected. "Unhand me!" he shouted when the two strapping young men who accompanied the Bosun took his arms. They didn't release him. People cheered as they hauled the banker off.

"This," Captain Wilson said to the assembled gamblers and ladies in the salon, as he handed the documents back, "is a letter of agreement for Duke Grangerford to acquire a collection of sacred objects belonging to Raven and sell them to a certain wealthy New Yorker. This, I believe, is in violation of several treaties, both with various Indian tribes and Mexico."

"What about the stolen chips?" Jim Douglas asked.

"Look there," Walker said, and strode toward the window through which Coyote and Raven had vanished. He plucked a sheet of paper from where it snagged on a splinter. Holding it up, he showed it to be a plan of the upper deck, with an "X" marked on a smokestack. "I suspect that's where the chips are hidden."

"I think you'll not have more problems with such thefts," Miss Kitty Belle said.

"Miss Kitty Belle, Mister Cheyenne Walker, I salute you for this. And, Mister Walker, you are welcome to resume your gaming. If you can find anyone willing to test themselves against you after the drubbing you gave Grangerford's wallet."

GOING AFTER YEECHIPHOOIE

SPAGHETTI!" HOWLED MAD COW BRAZOS WHEN HE SAW THE red-drenched strings Cookie slopped into his tin dish. "Spaghetti fer brekfas'? *Agin?!?!* "

"Sho' 'nuff beats jeller fer brekfas'," Hung Dawg Hooligan snarled from next to Brazos. "Out'n mah way, Ah'm hungered som'pin fierce."

Hooligan sharply elbowed Mad Cow in the ribs to move him from in front of the steaming vat from the stygian depths of which Cookie ladled his spaghetti. Mad Cow shot Hung Dawg a look that if it was from his .44 would have sprayed bits and pieces of bloody bones and gore over most of the visible landscape. Instead, he snarled and moved out of the way.

"It's 'cause som'un fergot t' load the beans 'n bacon onta the chuck wagon, " said Buzzard Bait Northrop, not to be confused with Buzzard Breath Northrop, to whom he was distantly related through his mother's second-cousin-twice-removed's side of the family.

Cookie's head jerked toward Buzzard Bait, the swarm of flies that constantly buzzed about his face seeking the effluvia that dripped into his beard when he tasted his cooking reorganized and followed his head so rapidly they hardly missed a drip. Thanks to the conscientious ministrations of the flies, Cookie had the cleanest beard of any of the cow-pokers, card-barracudas, and back-shooters who made up the posse searching for Yeechiphooie, the ancient Zinni god recently reincarnated and terrorizing the good folk of West Archaic, Arizona Territory.

"T'ain't mah fawlt!" Cookie snapped at Buzzard Bait. "Heavy Thumb Tromp dun gone 'n mis-labeled the barrels. Ah tol' him Ah wanted a mixed barrel o' pinto beans and great northerns. 'N tha's what the label on the barrel says. Yah kin see it fer yersef, ya wanna look." He faced front again and slopped a ladle-full of spaghetti and sauce into Hung Dawg Hooligan's dish. "If'n ya could read," he added softly, with a side-glance at Buzzard Bait Northrop.

"Ugh, me like'um spaghetti," Red Fork Wathahiya said loudly as he sidled up to the steaming vat. "Spaghetti sauce good! Look like clotted blood. *Taste* like clotted blood! Me like'um." Scorpion Stung Shaunessey and Buffalo Apple Cranston, who stood to Wathahiya's sides in the chuck line, edged away from the Injun.

Cookie shot Red Fork a dirty look but ladled an extra-large portion into his dish when he got to the head of the line, not only because Red Fork liked his cooking but because Wathahiya was the only Zinni who agreed to help the posse track down Yeechiphooie.

It began a month earlier when Thrown Shoe Hammerforge was woken by the panicked whinnying of the horses in his livery stable. He jumped out of bed in his nightdress and stocking cap, stepping directly into his carpet slippers, which were placed where they always were right where he could step into them if he had to suddenly rise in the middle of the night. Thus dressed, Thrown Shoe raced out of his house, which was situated immediately next to the stable, and saw to his wonder a six-foot-long arrow quivering in the front wall of the stable.

Before he could do anything about it, a hideous and hideously loud laugh attracted his attention. He looked to his left and *lo!* not two hundred yards away, standing in the light of the full moon, stood a ten-foot-tall Injun holding a bow! The Injun grinned at Hammerforge, showing teeth from which unspeakable oozings dripped from unutterable things caught between them and drew a threatening finger across his throat. With a thoroughly maniacal hideous and hideously loud laugh, the Injun disappeared. It was only then that Thrown Shoe realized the Injun hadn't cast a shadow in the brilliant moonlight!

A *whoosh* right next to Hammerforge caught his attention. The still-quivering arrow had burst into flames and the stable wall was catching on fire!

"*Far! FAR!*" Thrown Shoe shouted at the top of his lungs, and ran into the stable to open the stalls and lead the panicked beasts out.

In minutes, a dozen townsfolk were with him, leading the last of the cayuses out of danger and rounding up the frightened nags that had come out when nobody was yet there to corral them. None of the saddle or dray animals were lost, but the stable burned to the ground, and it was all the bucket brigade could do to keep the flames from devouring Hammerforge's house along with the stable.

No sooner had the livery stable been rebuilt than the mysterious Injun came back in the middle of the night and burned down Heavy Thumb Tromp's general store and the house where lived the good Parson Mather and his daughter Cassandra. The very night after the townsfolk got those two edifices rebuilt the dastardly and, the people were now thinking, probably supernatural Injun reappeared and burned down the Fat Chance Saloon, the Ante Up Gambling Hall, and Quick Cut's Barber Shop. The loss of the Fat Chance and the Ante Up rightly riled up the cow-pokers, card-barracudas, and back-shooters around West Archaic who relied on them for entertainment and (for the card-barracudas) income and the call rose for the sheriff to come from Archaic and do something about the situation.

Sheriff Shothip limped off the Ghoulhound Lines stagecoach three days later, saw all the new construction, and announced, "Don't look t' me like you got no problems heah," and got right back on the stagecoach and told the driver to turn around and take him back to Archaic. When the driver protested that he had a schedule to keep and was due in Shantak in two hours, which he'd never be able to do if he turned around and went back to Archaic now, Sheriff Shothip drew his Colt Peacemaker, pointed it at the driver, and said, "Ah said, take me back t' Archaic, mah business heah is finished," the driver said, "Yassah," and turned that stagecoach right around and headed back to Archaic, running down Little Billy Bonnie's puppy and almost trampling Old Miss Kitty in his haste to do the sheriff's bidding. (Little Billy Bonnie was so distraught at the untimely demise of his beloved puppy caused by Sheriff Shothip's haste to return to Archaic that he bore a lifelong disdain for the forces of law and order, and turned henceforth to banditry most foul.)

It was soon after that that Rybekka Ramrodder stood forth in the midst of West Archaic's main street (truth be told West Archaic's only street) and bellowed out in a voice to rattle the dead and possibly raise the recently dead, "Who heah's man enuff t' come with me and hunt that Injun down?"

For a while there it looked like no one was up to the challenge, that not another man was man enough to face the monstrous Injun who was terrorizing West Archaic. Rybekka Ramrodder began cursing and was about to turn away when Catastrophy Annie hitched up her bustle, gave the top of her bustier a yank, and stepped into the street. She walked up to Ramrodder and put a hand on his arm to stop him from leaving, then faced the crowds, withering like bushes in a draught. "If'n there's nobody *man* enough, mebbe there's some who is *wimmen* enough t' hunt thet Injun down!" she screeched.

Catastrophy Annie wasn't a rough-and-tumbler, and the only shooting iron she had any familiarity with was a dainty Derringer she kept in a holster on her wrist, under the sleeve of her dress. But she and her girls were having a hard time of it until the Fat Chance saloon got rebuilt. The only accommodations they'd been able to find during the reconstruction was the spare room in Parson Mather's new house. "Do you have any idea how *hard* it is to entertain customers in a *parson's* house?" she countered Zitz Fleiss when he demanded to know why business was off. "There's *five* of us and only *one* bed, so's we *cain't* entertain more 'n two at a time— if'n we kin sneak 'em past the parson. And when we do, that skinny dotter of his, that Cassandry, keeps poking her head in 'n shriekin' 'bout how disaster's comin'!" Catastrophy Annie didn't believe the supernatural Injun would stop bothering them once he burned down every building in West Archaic, but that he'd burn down the new buildings as well. She knew then she'd have to pack up and head for another town, and there just weren't that many empty cribs left in the Arizona Territory.

Her ploy worked, and soon enough Mad Cow Brazos, Hung Dawg Hooligan, Buzzard Bait Northrop, Sidewinder Calhoun, Ace Up His Sleeve Beauregard and enough other cow-pokers, card-barracudas, and back-shooters stepped up to form a right strong posse.

"Okay, Rebecca, how we gonna go after this Injun?" Skunk Beansworth asked when it was obvious nobody else was going to volunteer.

"Don't call me Rebecca!" Ramrodder roared. "It's *Rybekka!*" His eyes turned the red of hellfire, and the steam snorting out of his nostrils had a distinctly sulfurous tint in both color and stench.

"Whatever, Ramrodder," Scalped Hunter broke in before Ramrodder could draw down on Skunk Beansworth and reduce the size of the posse before they even got started. "What's yer idea fer catchin' this here Injun?"

It took visible effort for Ramrodder to get control of himself, but his eyes reverted to their normal bloodshot, and the steam from his nostrils became noticeably less sulphureous in both color and stench.

Finally, he looked down and kicked the dirt. "Ah shucks," he drawled. "Ah kind'a thunk mebbe one'a you would have an idea how t' do it. "

That was when the Zinni Injun Red Fork Wathahiya stepped out of the shadows where he'd stood observing and listening in his inscrutable Indian manner and said, "Me know how track 'im."

Everybody turned and stared at the unexpected apparition with his arms folded across his chest and a tomahawk dangling deadly from his belt. There were hushed murmurs of, "An Injun?" The scalped part of Scalped Hunter's head began bleeding at the sight of the Injun.

"Why not an Injun?" Catastrophy Annie screeched. "Gen'l Custer uses Crow Injuns t' track down the Sioux and Cheyanne all the time."

"Yeah, 'n look where it got 'im!" someone shouted out. It was August 4, 1876, and everybody knew what had happened at the Little Big Horn just a month earlier (though it seemed Catastrophy Annie didn't).

People started turning angry faces toward Red Fork Wathahiya.

The red man showed no fear. He unfolded his arms and raised one hand. "The Injun who comes to burn your wikkiups is Yeechiphooie. Yeechiphooie Anazinnijo heap-bad medicine. Long before pale eyes come, Yeechiphooie master-god of all Anazinnijo, keep Anazinnijo as slaves. Anazinnijo fight long time, finally drive Yeechiphooie into underground and all Anazinnijo live free until pale eyes come, turn Anazinnijo into Zinni shepherds, blanket weavers, and quaint native American dancers for entertainment of pale-eye tourists, and Japanese tourists who go around bothering people to pose with them for little pictures and buy kimchi dolls Zinni import from Korea. Me Zinni, used to be Anazinnijo. Me rather sell blankets and dance for pale-eye tourists, pose for little pictures with Japanese tourists and sell them kimchi dolls than be slave to Yeechiphooie. So me help you. "

"Well, what about the rest of them Zinni Injuns, they gonna help?" Buzzard Bait Northrup demanded.

Red Fork Wathahiya shook his head. "Other Zinni too afraid of Yeechiphooie. Most packing up, moving to Florida, wrestle alligators, sell turquoise jewelry to pale-eye tourists. "

Young Cassandra Mather, daughter of Parson Mather, stepped forward and shrieked, "You go to your doom!" But nobody backed out of the posse.

So it was that twenty intrepid souls, including Catastrophy Annie and the Zinni Injun Red Fork Wathahiya, headed out in search of Yeechiphooie and, after two weeks, found themselves having spaghetti for breakfast. *Again*. And back to our story.

They were halfway through eating, some few happily devouring the spaghetti in red sauce, some hungry enough they didn't care what they consumed, but most complaining about spaghetti *again*, when an eerie and most ominous fog swept in from nowhere. The members of the posse stopped eating and everybody looked up, trying in vain to pierce the dense, cloying, suffocating fog. Suddenly, a most hideous and hideously loud laugh sounded and madly rang and echoed manically off the surrounding spire rocks in such a chaotic manner that none of them could perceive from whence it came.

"That's him!" Thrown Shoe Hammerforge cried, his teeth chattering enough like a full Mariachi band of castanets to set a Spanish senorita to dancing. "He's north of us! "

"Tain't never no north o' us," Scalped Hunter cried back, his scalped scalp beginning to bleed once more just from hearing the laugh of the demented Anazinnijo god.

"Sou'east!" roared Keel Hauled Moby, who'd had enough of being a seaman and retired to arid Arizona to get away from ships, the sea, and fog.

"Due west!" insisted Ace Up His Sleeve Beauregard.

"Ever'body git yer shootin' arns out 'n git ready fer 'im!" Rybekka Ramrodder bellowed over everybody else.

"Gimme yer plates if'n you wants them clean fer lunch!" Cookie blabbered. He scampered about collecting the tin plates from everybody. His attendant cloud of flies briefly left their station before his face and beard to aid him in cleaning off the tin plates that he gathered.

Silence thudded like twenty bales of freshly plucked cotton bolls over the overnight camp of the posse, except for the clicking and clacking of the cow-pokers, card-barracudas, and back-shooters checking their arsenal of deadly weaponry to make sure everything was loaded and ready to blaze out with the balefire that would send Yeechiphooie back to whatever Dantean level of the ever-lasting inferno he'd come from.

Mad Cow Brazos opened the cylinder of his Navy Model 61 and critically eyed its loads. Satisfied that the primers looked good and were snugged firmly against the casing of his silver bullets, he snicked the cylinder closed and peered deep into the fog, which was so dense he couldn't see the front sight of the pistol he held arm's length in front of himself.

Hung Dawg Hooligan checked the points on the miniature stake (guaranteed to kill, or at least stop dead in his tracks, any vampire) in the chamber of his Henry, and put three more where he could grab them rapidly and reload.

Rybekka Ramrodder opened his Colt Junior Cadet, saw the glow, and quietly closed it again, only to be asked by Skunk Beansworth:

"What in tarnation is that green glow, Rebecca? "

"Don't call me Rebecca!" Ramrodder roared, the sulfurous steam from his nostrils only served to reduce the visibility in his vicinity to a foot and a half. But before he could say anything more a chorus of muffled *shhh*s came at him through the creeping, crawling, itching fog.

"Whatever," Beansworth whispered. "What's the green glow?"

"It's called kryptonite," Rybekka Ramrodder whispered harshly back.

"Wha's kryptonite?"

"Donno. It's green and it glows, and it's supposed to be able to stop super men daid in their tracks."

"Zat so? Well, I'll be. 'N here all I got fer my Sharps is holy water capsules, blest by the holy pope in Rome hisownself."

"I keep telling ya, it's my oil of vitriol that's gonna do in that Yeechiphooie critter," came Cookie's voice as from an impossible distance, as though he was being hauled away to a greater distance than they could imagine by some monster none of them wished to think about.

The hideous and hideously loud laugh came again accompanied by a mighty wind that swept the fog away, only to blow up so much dust and sand they had to close their eyes, though most of them didn't get their eyes closed fast enough to keep from getting grit stuck painfully under their eyelids.

The wind stopped as suddenly as it began and they heard a *THUNK!* like the cleaver of the devil's own headsman chopping through a neck into a chopping block.

As soon as the intrepid members of the posse could clear out their eyes, they looked at the chuck wagon to see a six-foot-long arrow quivering in its side.

"Oh no you don't!" Cookie screamed. He bounded out from his hiding place under the chuck wagon and latched both hands firmly on the shaft of the mighty magical arrow and yanked. The quivering arrow jerked him off his feet. When he got his balance back, he spat on his hands, wiped them vigorously on the seat of his canvas pants, and grabbed the arrow again. This time his cloud of flies gave him a hand, and he managed to extract the arrow a bare instant before it burst into a sun-rivaling blaze of fire.

"*YOW!*" Cookie screamed, dancing like the whole Hole in the Wall Gang was shooting at his feet, and waving his hands around to kill the flames, but to no avail as, while his hands were surely burned, they just as sure weren't burning!

The hideous and hideously loud bedlam laugh of the insane Zinni god came again, and this time there was no confusion where it was, it was directly beneath a massive thunder storm cloud closing in on them faster than they'd ever seen a cloud move before. Lightning shot down from the cloud, lighting up Yeechiphooie like a mysterious machine used by mad scientists trying to animate parts of dead bodies sewn together in awkward simulacrum of a person, followed almost immediately by a roll of thunder that knocked Cookie off his feet, as it did Catastrophy Annie and Buzzard Bait Northrop, who were speeding to the aid of the posse's cook.

Yeechiphooie laughed his hideous and hideously laugh once more and vanished from mortal sight.

Before anyone in the posse could even blink in wonder at the magical Injun god's vanishment the storm was upon them in all its fury. It was most fortunate none of them had pitched tents, if they had they would have had to spend days riding over half the Arizona Territory trying to find and retrieve their blown-away shelters. As it was, the only thing that saved the chuck wagon from being tumbled away by the mighty wind was the weight of the barrels labeled "Flour" but which in fact contained nothing but the red sauce Cookie cooked with the spaghetti from the barrels labeled "Pinto and Great Northern Beans."

The storm lasted only minutes, which was very fortunate, as the rain dropped so much water so fast that the cow-pokers, card-barracudas, and back-shooters were all completely soaked through. So much water came down from the sky that none of it had time to soak into the hardpan dirt before more came down, and the water that sluiced across the landscape rapidly deepened until, by the time the storm stopped after only minutes of deluge, the water was already more than ankle deep and sweeping away anything not heavy enough to resist the floodwater's force.

By the time the last of the flood dribbled away or percolated into the hardpan, and the posse rounded up everything important that the waters had swept away, it was lunch time.

"Jeller!" Mad Cow Brazos bellowed. "Jeller fer lunch? *AGIN!*"

"Gotta have the jeller," Cookie bellowed right back at him. "All that carnsarned rain got into the barrels labeled 'bacon' and wetted the jeller powder. So's we gotta eat it now b'fore it goes bad."

"Out'n mah way, Mad Cow," Hung Dawg Hooligan snarled. "Ah'm hungered som'pin fierce." He elbowed his way in front of Cookie and got his tin plate filled to the brim with red jeller with slices of cactus pear.

"Me like 'um jeller," Red Fork Wathahiya said from his place in line. "Look like blood. Taste like blood. Me like 'um." Scorpion Stung Shaunessey and Buffalo Apple Cranston, who stood to Wathahiya's sides in the chuck line, edged away from the Injun.

The cow-pokers, card-barracudas, and back-shooters of the posse grumbled, but ate their jeller, relieved that with the jeller powder wet they wouldn't have to eat much more of it.

When they finished eating, Red Fork Wathahiya stood and solemnly intoned, "Me know where Yeechiphooie went."

"Take us there," Rybekka Ramrodder snarled.

The lone Zinni Injun helping the posse pointed at a distant mountain. "There," he said in a voice that tolled of doom.

It took a day's hard riding for the posse to reach the foot of the mountain where Wathahiya showed them the entrance of a cave and told them that was where Yeechiphooie went.

"Why couldn't you brung us heah sooner?" Rybekka Ramrodder demanded.

"Me knew Yeechiphooie not home until now," Red Fork replied haughtily.

"Why you..." Buzzard Bait Northrop snarled and advanced on the red man with his hands balled into fists.

Sidewinder Calhoun, Scorpion Stung Shaunessey, and Buffalo Apple Cranston, blood in their eyes, loosened their shooting irons in their holsters and joined Buzzard Bait Northrop in closing on the Injun.

"Now you jest stop right there!" Catastrophy Annie shrilled, stepping in front of Wathahiya. She wagged a finger in the manner of a schoolmarm scolding recalcitrant boys in the faces of the cow-pokers and back-shooters bent on doing the Zinni bodily harm and chided them severely.

"If'n it warn't fer Red Fork heah, we wun't even know what we was up again', much less where t' find it!" she shrilled. "Now you jist *back* off 'n go 'bout yer business, 'n we'll git that there Yeechiphooie. "N that'll be thanks to this brave Injun here!"

Buzzard Bait Northrop unclenched his fists and looked down sheepishly, and Sidewinder Calhoun, Scorpion Stung Shaunessey, and Buffalo Apple Cranston did their best to look like they weren't following him.

"Ain't no purpose going inta that cave now," Rybekka Ramrodder announced. "Let's chuck down, git a good night sleep, and go in t' the cave in the mornin'." A chorus of agreement greeted the declaration.

"Chuck's ready!" Cookie shouted.

"Spaghetti!" Mad Cow Brazos roared when he saw the stringy, red-coated glop Cookie ladled into his tin plate.

"With a side o' jeller," Cookie said, slopping red jeller laced with tiny bits of a gila monster he'd just caught, killed, and gutted on top of the spaghetti in Mad Cow's tin dish. "Gotta git the jeller et while it kin still *be* et."

In the morning Rybekka Ramrodder distributed two pitch-headed torches to each of the seventeen who would enter the cave. He made Cookie stay outside with the chuck wagon over Cookie's protests, "Ah tell ya, it's mah oil of vitriol that'll do in thet Yeechiphooie!" Ramrodder also made Catastrophy Annie stay out, even though she insisted she was *more* able than any of the men were when he said she was too delicate to face the unknown horrors of the cave. Rybekka wasn't at all happy about leaving another man outside, but since Scalped Hunter's scalped scalp started bleeding again at the prospect of entering the Injun cave, he decided to have him stay outside to guard Catastrophy Annie and Cookie. Scalped Hunter didn't argue the point one bit.

"Light up ONE torch," Ramrodder ordered the sixteen cow-pokers, card-barracudas, back-shooters, and Red Fork Wathahiya, "'n keep yer other un fer when the first un burns out." They lined up at Cookie's cook fire and each lit only one torch under Rybekka's watchful eye.

Inside the cave, the flickering torches threw eerily dancing shadows over the riveletted walls and floor of the caves.

"Tarnation's thet?" Polecat Asskroft yelped when his torch lit up a scene of cabalistic Injun stick figures painted on the wall. The unsteady light of the torches made the stick figures seem to dance a wild and wooly war dance.

"Ugh," Red Fork Wathahiya rumbled when he pushed through the crowd to see what caught Polecat Asskroft's attention. "That heap old Anazinnijo med'cine. That chant-dance of Anazinnijo warriors, come drive Yeechiphooie deep inta cave. It work, too, Yeechiphooie not come back out for lo! these many moons from long time before pale eyes come."

Rybekka peered at the seemingly dancing stick figures, then looked suspiciously at Wathahiya. "Does that mean *we* gotta dance like 'em?"

The noble Zinni shook his head. "Dance only work for Anazin-nijo. Pale eyes try that dance, it make Yeechiphooie stronger."

Relieved, Rybekka wiped nervous sweat from his forehead, he wasn't a good dancer and didn't want to try to follow the complicated steps of the stick figures.

Their footsteps echoed hollowly as the seventeen continued into the depths of the earth, feeling with each step that they were descending ever deeper into the bowels of the Earth and if they kept going would eventually emerge blackened and wasted in China all the way on the other side of the world. They didn't go that far, though, before a hideous laugh even more hideously loud than any they had heard before stopped them, frozen to their cores with fear. Far ahead in the depths of the cave a faint glow appeared and slowly grew in size and brightness. After what felt like an eternity but in reality, was less than an hour, the light was so bright it drowned out the glow of their torches—and in the middle of the light stood the ten-foot-tall Injun god Yeechiphooie! He had a quiver of six-foot-long arrows slung over his shoulder and an eight-foot-long bow in his hand. Laughing a dementedly manic and hideous laugh Yeechiphooie drew an arrow, fitted it to his bow, and aimed it straight into the posse!

That was enough for them.

"RUN!" Skunk Beansworth screamed. "Rebecca, make 'em run afore we's all kilt!"

Don't call me Rebecca!" Rybekka Ramrodder roared and his roar was enough to jar the cow-pokers, card-barracudas, and back-shooters out of their unholy paralysis and start them running out of the cave. In their haste, they bowled Ramrodder over before his eyes turned full hellfire red and his snorting breath turned sulfurous in both color and stench. The leader of the posse leapt to his feet and followed the others out. All except Red Fork Wathahiya, the only man willing to stand and face the reincarnated Yeechiphooie.

Wathahiya began shuffling his feet and waving his arms in mimicry of the dancing feet of the Anazinnijo stick figures painted on the walls. His dancing worked for a time, and Yeechiphooie backed away, hiding his eyes behind his bent bow arm. But the evil god fought back until he was able to burst out with that hideous and hideously loud laugh. He gained strength and was able to stop backing away and hiding his eyes.

"Puny Anazinnijo brave," Yeechiphooie sneered. "You are strong, but one Anazinnijo brave is not enough to fend off the wrath of

Yeechiphooie!" And he notched the arrow he'd earlier drawn, drew his bow back, and shot. The six-foot-long arrow flew straight and true and struck Red Fork Wathahiya in the center of his breastbone, as though a bullseye had been drawn on the spot. It drove him back, skewering the noble savage flat against the cave wall in the midst of the dancing Anazinnijo stick figures. Then the ancient, evil god pranced after the hastily departed posse.

There was a great clangoring and thudding at the mouth of the cave when the cow-pokers, card-barracudas, and back-shooters of the posse ran smack dab straight into the chuck wagon, which Cookie, helped by Catastrophy Annie and Scalped Hunter had moved there.

"Careful there!" Cookie screamed. "Don't spill the oil of vitriol!"

"What in tarnation's goin' on heah?" Rybekka Ramrodder demanded when he made it to the mouth of the cave and saw the posse untangling itself and struggling to their feet.

"Dang people came crashing right out o' the cage 'thout look-ing where they was goin' and ran smack dab straight inta the trap Ah dun set fer that Injun god!" Cookie exclaimed.

Ramrodder looked at the chuck wagon stretched across the mouth of the cave and at the two barrels of oil of vitriol that perched precariously on its top and shook his head in wonder. "Do ya really think that'll work?" he asked.

Cookie looked at the people still unheaping themselves, listened to the approaching prance of Yeechiphooie, and said, "It better or we's in big trouble. Now hep me git these people out'n the way!"

Rybekka Ramrodder pitched in and they had everyone cleared out of the way right before Yeechiphooie switched from a prance to a charge and roared out of the cave—smack dab straight into the chuck wagon.

A charging ten-foot-tall evil Anazinnijo god carries a humungous amount of momentum, and Yeechiphooie's momentum was enough to dislodge the barrels of oil of vitriol from their unsteady perch atop the chuck wagon. They crashed down, dumping their contents on the reincarnated god.

The immortal Yeechiphooie screamed in mortal agony when the oil of vitriol slopped over his body. He swiped at it with his hands in futile attempt to brush it away, but every swipe of his huge hands merely served to spread the deadly oil further onto untouched parts of his body. Steam rose where the bubbling oil of vitriol ate at his flesh, turning it into molten gunk that dripped and spattered to the rocky ground. In moments, all that was left of Yeechiphooie was his gurgling scream, and even that didn't last much longer.

There was silence for a time as the cow-pokers, card-barracudas, and back-shooters looked at the unholy and sickly mess on the rocks where the terror of West Archaic had just met his grisly demise.

"Whar's Red Fork Wathahiya?" Catastrophy Annie finally asked. "We owe him a big thanks. And Cookie, too."

Rybekka Ramrodder looked at the cave entrance, and the spreading puddle of gunk in front of it that he knew no man could cross alive and said, "I heard him dancin' that Anazinnijo dance b'hind me. I think he died givin' the rest o' us time ta git out'n the cave."

"We'll put up a memorial ta him in the town square," Buzzard Bait Northrop said, wiping a tear from his eye.

"Ta him and Cookie," Mad Cow Brazos said, draping an arm over Cookie's shoulder.

And so, the town of West Archaic was saved from the evil Anazinnijo god Yeechiphooie.

ROCKY ROLLS GOLD

VLANCH ROLLED HIS SHOULDERS IN A NOT-QUITE SHRUG; IT sounded like boulders grinding together. "What can we do?" he asked in a gravel-pit voice that somehow managed to sound plaintive.

Grubble shook her head, a boulder pinging down a rocky slope. "You claim you're the smart one," she said in a voice not as gravel-pitty as Vlanch's, more like a shaken sack of pebbles. "You tell me what we can do."

He blinked at her; if the lids that scraped across his eyeballs had been steel, they would have struck sparks. "You heard the dwarf. If we go back there, it will not go well for us." He raised his left arm to display the light streak where a blow from the pick wielded by the dwarf leader had gouged his side. He knew the dwarf had meant to only scratch him that time.

"But you promised me gold and gems!" Grubble squealed, a granite spike scraping down a sheet of slate.

"And I will get you gold for your birthday, and gems for our anniversary," he rumbled. Then, in a voice like sand sliding on a gentle grade, "Just not from the dwarves." He looked down the mountainside, past the green band where trees girded its loins, to the red gash in the ground just above where the mountain turned to plain. A red line where men had recently finished constructing one of their aboveground caves, a place that was quickly vanishing as men planted greenery and laid out roads and walkways.

Another line of barren ground, angling down the mountainside until it passed nearly a mile north of the hotel, was the trackway of an avalanche, dotted by boulders, large, medium, but mostly small, and kept clear of new trees and shrubs by the passage of an occasional freshly tumbling boulder.

Vlanch ignored the copse of thin, mirrored towers that rose offset to one side of the structure, which he knew stood very nearly atop the dwarven gold mine they'd been forced from. Instead, he looked at the swath of forest that backed against the hotel, and the rock-strewn ground above the trees. A plan began to form in his mind.

Vlanch and Grubble squatted in that trackway, looking like nothing so much as two piles of boulders, one slightly larger than the other. A casual viewer looking in their direction might wonder at boulders piled thusly. But nobody looked that way.

⟶•◖◗•⟵

A green-eyed woman with an ivory complexion and ruby lips stood at the check-in desk of the Glittering Nugget Hotel; two traveling trunks and a carpetbag sat on the floor at her side. She was in obvious disagreement with the clerk, who opposed her from the far side of the counter.

"You cannot deny a woman a room simply because she is traveling unaccompanied," she stated firmly. "Especially not when she has wired ahead to reserve a room. I have been so looking forward to this holiday, too much so to allow an impertinent clerk to disturb it."

"Madam," the clerk said haughtily, "the Glittering Nugget Hotel has its reputation to consider. Unaccompanied women checking into a hotel are often... well, I don't wish to be indelicate. But I cannot let you have a room. I'm certain you can find suitable quarters elsewhere, perhaps in the workers' lodging." A smirk graced his visage.

Danger flared in the woman's green eyes, and she parted her lips to verbally lash the impertinent clerk when a man in a newly cleaned frock coat stepped to the counter and spoke to her.

"Miss Kitty Belle!" he said with clear delight, and raised fingers to his brow, as though touching the brim of a hat.

She turned her face to him. "Why, so I am, Mister Cheyenne Walker," she said, with a slight nod of her head.

"Is Mister Reghaster causing you distress about your registration?" Walker asked.

"Not as much distress as I shall cause *him* if he doesn't promptly honor my reservation!"

Walker slowly shook his head. "I'd rather you didn't. It's so hard to find clerks proficient in the operation of the Babbage Analytical Engine."

"This hotel has a Babbage Analytical Engine?" she asked, with obvious surprise. When Walker replied in the affirmative, she turned to the clerk. "I want to see it in operation," she demanded.

"But—" he said uncertainly and looked to Walker. Walker simply smiled softly.

"And what might your position be here? Surely, you're not the manager," she asked Walker while observing the clerk clack fingertip levers to make a punch card.

A sound like teapot-whistle emitted from beneath the counter. "Are you brewing chai?" she demanded of Reghaster.

"That is the engine that provides the motive power for the Babbage," the clerk replied haughtily.

Walker ignored the byplay and answered her original question. "I have a table in the salon, and share my winnings with the hotel."

"And how often are you challenged?"

Walker laughed. "Never! Ever since the incident on the *Samuel Clemens*, I remove my coat and pull up my shirtsleeves before I game. None can claim I slip hidden cards into my hand." Miss Kitty well recalled their sojourn on the paddlewheeler and could not fault him his caution.

"Miss?" Reghaster interrupted them. "This," he held up the card he'd just punched, "will show whether you have a reservation." He inserted the card into an orifice in the machine, clacked a lever, and stepped back. "Now we wait for a moment." He sounded like he thought finding a reservation wouldn't change matters. The teapot whistle increased in volume.

A new clacking sounded from within the machine, and another punch card poked out of a different orifice. Reghaster removed the new card to another machine, inserted it, and again stepped back. The second machine began teapot-whistling and clacking with slender arms that slapped out of a well in its center onto a sheet of paper.

"That looks ever so much like one of those typing machines on which Mister Twain writes his humorous books!" Miss Kitty Belle exclaimed.

"Yes, it's been modified for automatic writing," Reghaster said with a sniff. The clacking stopped and he whipped the sheet of paper from the machine and looked it over. His expression of superiority quickly vanished as he read, and he ran a finger around the inside of his collar.

"Miss, this says your registration was made by Mister Pinkerton himself." He cleared his throat. "Would that be *the* Mister Pinkerton?"

She smiled at him.

"Oh, dear." He read farther and said again, "Oh, dear. There is a note appended to the reservation, a note from Colonel Gimble, to accord you every courtesy."

"Colonel Gimble owns the Glittering Nugget, along with other establishments in the territory," Cheyenne Walker said in answer to Kitty Belle's eloquently raised brow.

After confirming the reservation—and again reading the note from his employer—Reghister's fingers veritably danced over the levers of the Babbage Analytical Engine, causing the teapot-whistle to sing merrily. After a moment—somewhat longer than the one it had taken to discover Miss Kitty Belle's reservation—a card poked out of the same orifice as the reservation had.

"Ah, Miss Belle, I do wish to apologize for the misunderstanding earlier, and to make amends," Reghaster said. "To that end, I can," his eyes skimmed the card, "I can put you in a suite. Not, of course, the bridal suite—" he blushed at that mention, "but certainly a suite superior to the simple bed-sitting room your reservation requires." He shot an embarrassed glance at Cheyenne Walker. "That is, naturally, at no additional charge to either you or to your employer." He briskly tapped the bellhop's bell and turned to fetch the key to the suite he was assigning to her.

Cheyenne Walker accompanied Miss Kitty Belle as she followed the bellhop. Her luggage was in the bellhop's care.

"Mister Walker, the whistling of the Babbage Analytical Machine," she asked, "is it steam-operated, as were the great wheels on the *Samuel Clemens*?"

"It is indeed. As were the fans that propelled the *Argus*, and as is the Otis that will convey you to the ninth floor."

"The ninth floor." She shook her head in wonder. Such a tall building would barely be possible were it not for Mister Otis and his marvelous lifting apparatus.

"Ah, but the Glittering Nugget has *twelve* floors." Walker sounded so pleased with twelve floors that a casual over hearer might be forgiven for assuming that he was the proprietor.

An elevating room was waiting when they reached its lobby, where Cheyenne Walker and Miss Kitty Belle parted company.

He gave the Pinkerton agent a slight bow and asked, "Might I have the pleasure of your company at dinner this evening?"

"I would be displeased if you didn't desire it, Mr. Walker," she answered with a smile and a dip of her head.

"Will six o'clock suffice?"

"Let us make it half past."

"Half past six it is. Until then."

Vlanch kept a cautious eye toward the immediate environs of the Glittering Nugget, watching for any who might see him and Grubble as they slowly made their way toward the bordering trees. He knew that their forms would look to a man like nothing so much as two jumbles of rocks: a careful observer might notice that their parts maintained their relative positions, or that they were moving in defiance of Galileo's gravity law, that they didn't move toward the center of the Earth, but rather sideways, toward the edge of the trackway. And even a bit uphill.

But he saw no one looking their way, not even with the most casual of glances, much less the lingering look required to see their non-Galilean movement.

And he knew that the men in the aboveground cave possessed gold and gems. If the cave were shattered, he could get into it and find that gold and those gems, keeping his promise to his mate.

They kept up their cautious movement.

Half past six found Cheyenne Walker ensconced at a table that gave him a clear view of the entrance to Placer's Poke, the Glittering Nugget's dining salon. His wait for Miss Kitty Belle wasn't excessively long, merely long enough to pique his appetite for her company.

When she arrived, the *maitre'd* bowed her in like visiting royalty; he seemed nearly overwhelmed by her glory.

Walker stood as if physically drawn to his feet. "You look spectacular, Miss Kitty Belle," he said, his gaze traveling appreciatively over her brocaded skirt of crimson arabesques on a field of ebony. He liked that there was no bustle, and the way her jacket was patterned in reverse of the skirt's coloring. It hung open down the front framing the pale pink of a ruffled blouse. The jaunty angle of the hat cocked on her crown teased a smile from Walker's lips. Brilliant feathers cascaded from one side of the hat, and the opposing, higher, brim was speckled with seashells. He added his bow to that of the *maitre'd*.

"And you, Cheyenne Walker," she said as she eased onto the chair drawn back for her by a waiter, taking in Walker's freshly brushed frock coat, ruffled shirt, and string tie held beneath his chin by an onyx clip, "look quite dashing yourself."

On the *maitre'd's* recommendation, she had quail in puff pastry, and Walker ordered pheasant with figs. They shared a bottle of sauvignon blanc.

Once sated, they engaged in small talk over coffee. Until she said casually, "I heard a rumor that an engineer on a routine inspection of the steam works vanished. Have you heard about that?"

Walker cocked his head. "I thought you were on holiday."

"I am. But a detective can't help but overhear things and wonder about them."

He shrugged. "I also have heard that rumor. I've also heard that the engineer, by name of Hyram Scott, was later seen in the Yellowstone territory spending gold and attempting to sell diamonds. And I heard he was doing the same at the same time in Dodge City, Kansas."

"Well! And where might he have found gold and diamonds?"

"Not from any of the guests here. At least, none have reported such a theft. Neither was the security of the hotel's safe breached."

Miss Kitty looked out the window, at the climbing face of the Front Range behind the hotel. "Gold has been found in many places in Colorado. It could be that there is gold near here."

"And a dwarven gold mine?"

Her eyes went unfocused for a moment, then she said, "I've long been fascinated by the workings of steam. Do you think I could visit the steam room?"

"Certainly. I'm sure the hotel's manager will allow us to examine the basement." Although he did wonder about her sudden change of topic.

"Sir," An attendant interrupted, leaning in to whisper into Walker's ear.

"Thank you. I'll be right there." Walker rose to his feet and essayed a bow to his dinner companion. "I fear duty calls, Miss Kitty. My table awaits me, along with gamblers who wish to attempt to divest me of my money. Shall we meet again for breakfast, and then hence to the sub-levels?"

She tipped her head and graced him with a smile. "I'm sure you will be able to pay for both our breakfasts."

The din of the steamworks grew from almost inaudible to nearly deafening as Cheyenne Walker and Miss Kitty Belle descended a long flight of stairs tucked away behind the accounting office. There were whistles and clanks and pings and pops; all the sounds of metal expanding and contracting as it heated and cooled, containing the steaming-hot water it directed from boilers to destinations through pipes. All of which had welded valve joints that sometimes, Walker knew and Kitty Belle suspected, sprang leaks.

Chief Engineer James Bankey, who had been alerted by the manager to expect visitors, met them in a small, gas-lit anteroom at the foot of the stairs. Conversation was possible so long as one spoke in a loud voice.

"Mr. Walker, Miss Belle," Bankey said, giving them a satisfied look. So often visitors came clad in their holiday finery, such clothing destined to be ruined by the oil and dirt and steam beyond the anteroom. These two, at least, wouldn't complain about the state of their clothes after they left: Walker wore a canvas overcoat and trousers, and Kitty Belle a well-worn denim skirt and matching jacket, much more suitable clothing for their visit. "I've been instructed to accord you every consideration," he said as though delivering a rote presentation. "So, I can, for a short time, spare Thomas, one of our apprentices, to escort you about and answer your questions—to the best of his necessarily limited ability, him being only an apprentice." He indicated a sturdy young man standing at his left shoulder. "Is this satisfactory?"

"It is more than satisfactory, Mr. Bankey," Walker said. "We had thought we might have to stumble through your environs unguided and be abjectly ignorant of what we looked on," he jibed, suspecting Bankey would rather visitors wandered unattended provided they didn't touch anything.

Bankey snorted. "Not likely I'd allow civilians to traipse about my workings and get into who knows what mischief.

"But since I must," he grudgingly added, "you had best wear these." He reached into a pocket of his grease-stained overalls and drew out two sets of ear mufflers. "Without these, it might be hours after leaving here before you can hear normally again." After adjusting the mufflers on Walker and Kitty Belle, he resumed his own, as did the apprentice.

"Now, Thomas," he said in an even louder voice, one that sounded through the mufflers as from a distance, or penetrating a dense fog, "take good care of our guests."

Beyond the foyer, the din was so great that the mufflers hardly seemed to reduce the noise. Walker quickly saw that some of the sunlight funneling into the cavernous space was deflected to an array of mirrors on the ceiling, reflecting it to bathe the space with light.

"How do we not hear this inside the hotel?" Miss Kitty shouted, leaning close to Cheyenne Walker's ear.

He leaned close to her ear and shouted, "It's not directly under the hotel. It's under the sun-towers."

She didn't strain her voice replying, merely nodded as she recalled the group of parabolic-mirrored towers such as she'd seen in other locations—only not so many together. Indeed, they stood at a slight distance from the hotel. The earth would absorb the sound and vibrations of the steamworks. She remembered that the mirrors captured the rays of the sun and focused them to heating mirrors under the boilers. One tower for each boiler, she assumed.

While there was space around each boiler to allow easy access for the engineers who tended them, elsewhere passages were tight, and people moving from one place to another sometimes brushed against hot pipes, scorching their clothing or smearing grease on them. Cheyenne Walker and Miss Kitty Belle were no exception. It wasn't long before she looked at her sleeves and skirt and decided she'd likely have to discard the garments after this expedition. A penetrating glance told her that though Walker's coat and trousers suffered more than her clothing, they were of a sturdier material than hers, and would more likely survive the steamworks to be worn another day.

Thomas didn't attempt to talk to them, but rather contented himself with gestures, and tracing patterns in the air. Probably describing the inner working of the steam in the pipes.

The wending path the apprentice led them on eventually reached a wall, where the constant din was less. Walker drew him close and asked about the stony nature of the wall.

Still signing rather than strain his voice, Thomas indicated that the basement was dug into bedrock. Nodding his understanding, Walker then asked if Thomas had known Hyram Scott. When the apprentice nodded, Walker asked if he knew what had happened to the man. Thomas spread his hands in an I-don't-know gesture.

"Where was he last seen?" Kitty Belle shouted.

Thomas looked into the distance, then waved a "follow-me." He led them to another section of the bedrock wall, where he again spread his hands, this time with a shrug.

Before either of them could ask who had been the last person to see Scott, a whistle, far louder than any they'd heard before, blasted through the steamworks. Thomas' eyes and mouth popped wide, and he signed them to stay put, then dashed off.

"I think we should find our way out," Walker mouthed, but Miss Kitty wasn't looking at him. Instead, she was staring at the wall they stood next to. Walker's eyes followed her gaze.

The bedrock here had been disturbed.

There was a filigree of cracks in the face of the rock. In a couple of places, flakes had chipped off, so the cracks seemed to be wider under the surface than on it.

Walker drew a folding knife from a pocket of his coat and used its blade to pry a flake from one of the cracks. Not only was the crack wider under the surface, there was what looked to be a foreign, whitish substance inside it, bulging toward the surface. He used the point of his blade to scrape off a little of the substance and touched it to his tongue.

He leaned close to Miss Kitty and said loudly, "Lime." Someone had used cement to seal the cracks—from the inside!

Walker removed the muffler from his right ear and pressed it against the cracked surface. Miss Kitty did the same. They exchanged astonished looks.

While they were considering the cemented cracks that widened beneath the surface, and the sounds they'd heard from beyond it, Thomas reappeared and waved at them to follow him. In a few moments he had them back at the entrance to the cellar.

Inside it, the apprentice said his first words to them. "Mr. Bankey hopes you enjoyed your visit. Now it's time for you to leave." He held out his hands to receive the mufflers they'd worn. As soon as he had them, he left the two with nothing to do but climb the long flight back to the ground floor of the Glittering Nugget.

Upon gaining the ground floor, they retired to their own rooms to refresh and change into clean clothes, agreeing to meet again in the Placer's Poke. They were shown to a table in an alcove, where they were unlikely to be overheard by other diners. They waited until the bread and cheese plate they ordered was served before they began talking about what they'd seen—and heard.

"Ladies first. What did you hear?" Walker said, daubing mustard on bread for a chunk of cheese.

"It didn't sound like the sea in my ear, like a conch shell makes," she said. "There was a faint two-tone beat, a sort of high-low, repeated in different registers." She shook her head at the memory.

"Punctuated by faint *clinks*, as a pick might make striking stone," Walker said.

She nodded. "Most peculiar," she agreed.

"Did you notice the patterning of the cracks?"

She poked her fork at chunks of cheese while remembering the face of the wall. "Again odd. It was as though the wall had been reassembled."

"After having been broken through from the other side." He peered unfocused into a never-never for a long moment, before slowly saying, "There are old legends of dwarves mining for gold and gems in the front range. But the legends always put them in remote locations where hardly anybody ever goes. Certainly, no place where a white man ever stumbles across them. I wonder if it's possible that dwarves are mining here."

Miss Kitty Belle looked at Cheyenne Walker and nodded sagely. "I suspect that on the other side of that repaired wall, there just might be a dwarven mine."

"Do you think that's even remotely possible?" he asked, surprised.

She shrugged. "I don't advise opening that wall to find out. The little I've heard of dwarves, they seem disinclined to welcome visitors to their mines."

Vlanch and Grubble, still moving slowly, had at length penetrated the forest at the edge of the avalanche trackway and were working their way to a spot directly above the Glittering Nugget Hotel. They increased their speed and headed uphill, aiming for a field of boulders above the trees. Particularly for a giant boulder that perched just above the beginning of a knife-edge ridge that plunged a short distance down the slope.

On the morrow, Miss Kitty Belle and Cheyenne Walker joined an expedition of hotel guests for a picnic high on the slope above the hotel. On preparing to leave his room, Walker had glanced at his Gladstone bag, in which his Buntline Special revolver was stored. A second's consideration told him neither grizzly bear nor mountain lion would attack a sizable party, so he had no need of it.

The group consisted of some ten vacationers, led by a mountain guide named Beavertrap Jackson, and accompanied by a small coterie of hotel staff bearing food, drink, dinnerware, and silver, as well as tablecloths on which to lay out the provisions. It was cool under the trees. Not bracingly, but cool enough that there was little perspiration dripping off the group of mostly flat-landers. The slow amble at which they climbed aided in keeping them relatively dry. After a walk of close to an hour and a half, they reached a patch of nearly level ground where rustic tables and benches had been erected to receive the cloths and provisions.

"So much for roughing it," someone in the group quipped, which elicited relieved laughter from most of the group.

"This hike has been roughing it enough for me," another offered.

The porters, who made this trek weekly, set about covering the tables and benches with the blankets, and laying out the picnic. The meal was cold cuts on bread, salads, with sarsaparilla as the beverage. The picnickers made short work of it.

Someone had brought a ball, and after the meal the men tossed it around while the women clustered together to chat.

When it came time to head back downhill, Cheyenne Walker and Miss Kitty Belle decided to stay behind and explore farther up the mountainside. They needed to talk more about what they'd discovered—or thought they'd discovered—in the hotel's steam-works. If there actually was a dwarvish gold mine, they might be able to find its entrance. Although what they'd do if they found it, they didn't know.

Half a mile up they came across...

"How strange," Walker said. "Strange that two piles of small boulders would be within the trees without a trackway to show how they came to this place; and strange that they roughly resemble human forms."

"Someone must have put them there," Kitty Belle said brightly. "But let's not tarry." She grasped his arm and continued rapidly uphill.

He looked at her curiously but went without protest.

⟡⟡⟡

"Do you think they recognized us?" Grubble asked.

"How could they?" Vlanch replied. "They never saw us before."

Grubble playfully punched his shoulder, sending a cascade of sand down his arm. "Not *us*, silly. I mean our kind."

"They said nothing."

"That means nothing."

"We should have killed them?"

"We still should kill them."

"Then let us follow them."

They resumed their slow, upward trundle.

⟡⟡⟡

A quarter mile beyond, Miss Kitty Belle stopped and peered at their backtrail. Speaking softly, hardly more than a whisper, she said, "I think those were rock trolls. Let's keep going."

"Rock trolls?" Walker asked. "I've never heard of them."

"They are trolls that appear to be made of rock. They are slow moving, but are nonetheless very strong, and can be extremely violent. Let us be sure to avoid them on our return."

They walked more briskly, and soon came to the high treeline at the peak of the knife-edge ridge.

Walker said, "They might have something extremely violent in mind, if they're what you say." All thoughts of finding the entrance to the dwarven mine were driven from his mind by the approaching threat. "If they can move that big one and send it down the ridge rather than sliding off its side, I think they might be able to start an avalanche that would smash directly into the hotel. But why would they do that?"

"They would," a harsh voice said, "because they're thieves, an' they wants gold."

Walker and Miss Kitty spun toward the voice.

"Who's there?" Walker demanded when he saw no one. His hand reached for the side of his coat before he remembered that he left his Buntline Special locked in his room. "You also, I see," Miss Kitty murmured. Her Colt Peacemaker was likewise locked securely in her room.

A stout man, only chest-high to Walker, stepped from behind a boulder the size of a cottage. A bushy beard covered his face below a bulbous nose, and eyebrows so thick they nearly hid his eyes. A red, tasseled stocking cap lounged atop his head. A green, homespun jerkin was belted with a length of leather, and brown homespun trousers on his bandy legs were tucked into scuffed boots with steel caps on their toes.

"The rock trolls," the apparition said, "already tried to steal from us and we sent them off. But why would they want t' destroy yon hotel?"

"Maybe to get to the hotel's safe?" Walker said uncertainly.

"'Tis of no mind to us if they do. But ye, ye *are* of a mind to us. We saw ye looking at the place where poor Hyram Scott found the break into our mine shaft afore we could repair it. Then he had the misfortune t' enter the mine." The dwarf shook his head sadly. "He's been slavin' fer us ever since. Ye would'na be thinking o' following him, would ye?"

"I think that would be highly unwise of us," Walker said to the dwarf. In an aside to Miss Kitty, he added, "So, Scott is in neither Yellowstone nor Dodge city."

"That 'tis good thinking on yer part. Ye would'na want t' join Mr. Scott in slavin' fer us, now. That would be a most uncomfortable fate to suffer. I'll be taking me leave o' ye now." He doffed his cap and turned to go.

"A moment, Mister dwarf," Miss Kitty called. "It might be of mind to you if the rock trolls destroy the hotel."

"Oh? An' why might that be?" the dwarf asked, turning to face her.

"Because if the hotel is destroyed, there will certainly be an investigation. That investigation will most assuredly find your mine shaft."

"Ye think so, do ye? An' why would that be?"

"I am a Pinkerton. You know what that is, don't you?"

He screwed up his face and peered at her. "A Pinkerton, eh? Can ye prove it?"

She reached into a pocket and withdrew a leather wallet, which flipped open to show her badge.

"Well, well. So ye are, it appears. An' ye would know about an investigation? An' what if ye were killed in the avalanche, an' could'na tell any about the mine?"

"In that case, the Pinkertons would be most anxious to investi-gate—and avenge, if needed—the death of one of their agents. And be assured, they would find your mine."

"So ye say, so ye say. Hmmm." The dwarf twined his fingers into his beard, tugging on it, lost in thought.

After a moment that ended before it became long enough to grow uncomfortable, the dwarf peered up at them through his bushy brows. "So ye say t'would be to our advantage t' prevent the trolls from raining boulders down 'pon the hotel."

"Yes, it would be highly advantageous to you," she said, press-ing her edge.

"I'll gi' help." The dwarf spun about and disappeared with a *pop* of displaced air.

"It would be an interesting job to catch him," Walker said after a few seconds.

"T'would be interesting to *try*, anyway," Miss Kitty said. "Although I'm not sure we could, given his ability to vanish."

"What's that?" Walker suddenly snapped, twisting to look downslope.

"Oh, no," Miss Kitty exclaimed. "Could it be the rock trolls already?"

It could and it was.

Fifty yards away, they saw a slender tree crash to the ground, its trunk smashed by a blow from one of the stony creatures.

"Oh, my," Kitty Belle said.

A rumbling came from downslope, noise like boulders grinding together, and a gravel pit stirred by a gigantic ladle. They saw indistinct gray forms moving through the foliage and shadows and heard more crashes as the trolls in their haste knocked down more trees.

"Run!" Walker shouted. Grabbing Miss Kitty's hand, he stepped to the right, and immediately turned to step to the left.

"What way do we go?" Miss Kitty shouted.

The ridge was so narrow between its precipitous sides they'd have to brush past at least one of the nearing rock trolls to get past them, or risk plummeting over the edge.

"Uphill!" Walker shouted at the same time Miss Kitty cried out, "Climb!"

They scrambled, increasing the distance between themselves and the trolls, who were now climbing at the speed of a walking man. Past the large boulder they paused to consider their next move.

Miss Kitty looked at the ground ahead of them, and at her boots. The otherwise barren ground was speckled too thickly with small rocks, ranging from baseball-size to fine gravel, to leave open spaces for her to step securely. The soles of her boots were narrow, and her heels were a full inch and a half in height, fine for walking on the leaf-litter under the trees, but not for climbing.

Walker saw and looked at the huge boulder. It rose vertically nearly fifteen feet above the ground. He said, "Up. I doubt that they can mount this boulder."

"I think you're right," Miss Kitty said, looking at the side of the knobs and indentations on the rocky face. "But the first handholds are too high for me to reach."

"Here," he said, lowering a knee and offering his hands as a stirrup.

"Yes!" She stepped into his hands and straightened as he did likewise. She stretched. "Not quite, I need a couple more inches."

He let go of her foot with one hand, placed it where she wasn't wearing a bustle, and pushed.

"Sir, your hand!" she yelped. But that gave her the extra height she needed to grasp a knob to pull herself farther. "I can make it from here. But what about you?"

"Keep climbing." He backed away and anxiously watched as she clambered upward. When she was far enough, he sprinted forward and jumped, planting one foot on the face of the rock, to vault high enough to grasp the first protuberance. He pulled up, and soon clambered high enough that his face was next to her ankle.

In seconds more, just as the rock trolls reached its base, they were atop the bulging peak of the cottage-size boulder.

"Now what do we do? They are too high for us to reach," Grubble wailed.

Vlanch considered the situation for a moment, then said, "You stay here in case they try to come down. I'm going around to the other side and dig out in front of it. Then we will push and make this rock roll. And this stone will tumble down to smash into the man-cave so we can get to the gold it hides—and crush the two men on top of it as it rolls."

"You are so smart, Vlanch!"

Miss Kitty flung herself down on the boulder's top, head downs-lope. "Hold my ankles," she ordered, and slithered forward so she could see what the noise was she heard from the downhill direction. "This wasn't a good idea," she said when she saw the rock troll shoveling its stony hands into the earth at the foot of the boulder. "He's digging it out on that side so it'll roll."

"The other one is guarding the back side," Walker said. He stood and looked around, seeking a way to the ground that would avoid the two rock trolls. The only way he saw, to one side, risked a twisted ankle, or worse. "We're trapped," he shouted.

And no sooner had he said that than a wild *harroo* sounded from many voices, and a flurry of small, stocky men in homespun boiled out of… of… of *somewhere* and attacked the two rock trolls.

The dwarves were armed with picks and sledges, mauls and chisels, rakes and shovels, hammers and drills. One had an oyster rake, of all things, and Walker couldn't imagine what another intended to do with the broom and coal scuttle he bandied about.

The dwarves hopped and leapt and skittered about the two rock trolls, distracting them from their fronts and striking them from behind, mostly skipping just out of reach when the trolls turned about to get at their tormentors. Here and there, now and then, one of the trolls' flailing arms connected with a dwarf, sending it flying, broken and spraying blood.

All the while the dwarves kept up a frightful *harroo* and skirl, even in the absence of pipes. Each time they connected, sparks flew from the trolls, and pebbles and sand were flung off their sides or fronts, or wherever they were hammered.

The rock trolls shouted, the roars of twin avalanches. They swung their mighty arms, digging divots in the hard earth and stone of the rock-strewn ground. They backhanded the boulder with flesh-and-bone-crushing blows. With every strike of pick, sledge, maul, chisel, hammer, drill, every flinging of pebbles and sand, the rock trolls shrank in size.

And they shrank and shrank and grew smaller by the stroke.

The rock trolls were backed against the boulder, and their mighty—though diminishing—arms flew side to side with greater urgency, always seeking a dwarvish target, which was never there when their granite hands reached their targets. But often their swinging fists struck the boulder hard enough that had it been metal, it would have rung like a Gothic cathedral's entire bell tower of bells. Which caused the boulder to twitch and tremble and threaten to topple.

At length, the rock trolls were beaten so they were no larger than the dwarfs, at which point the maul and chisel-armed dwarves closed on them and sundered their limbs, hand from forearm, forearm from shoulder, foot from ankle, shin from thigh, head from neck, neck from chest, chest from belly. Others grasped the pieces and flung them over the sides of the narrow ridge, where they tumbled down, cracking and splitting as they fell.

The dwarf who had first appeared to Cheyenne Walker and Miss Kitty Belle looked over one side and briskly brushed his hands against each other. "I told ye, ye'd come to no good end if ye again tried to take our gold."

"Ah, some help here, if you please?" Cheyenne Walker called down from the now-swaying boulder top.

The dwarf leader looked at the two people, his eyes metronomically following their movement. Then his look shifted to the boulder itself, and he realized the movement was in the stone, not the people—and the swaying was increasing. He shouted a rapid command to his companions, and they scrambled to his side. Then to Walker and Miss Kitty. "Jump, we'll catch you!"

Walker looked at the mass of little people. He thought he could probably make the jump uninjured without their help, and sufficiently break Miss Kitty's fall. But if the dwarves could be trusted to catch them, both of them would be safe.

Miss Kitty made the decision. "Ready, I'm coming!" she shouted and dove, arms spread, and body parallel to the ground. Eager arms reached out to cradle her and stop her fall before she hit the ground.

"Your turn," she called to Walker as soon as she gained her feet.

He manfully followed her example, and the sturdy arms of ten dwarves reached out and held as he plopped into them.

With both on their feet and unharmed, the head dwarf stood before them, arms akimbo.

"Ye recall what I said about poor Hyram Scott, and the consequences of following him?"

"Yes, we do," Walker said. "We will not follow him."

"And the Pinkertons now have no need to investigate," Miss Kitty added.

"Ver' good." He turned to his troop. "Let's be off, high-low!"

There was a sudden rumble, and the earth shook as the boulder finally rocked too far, and began to roll downhill, heading straight for the Glittering Nugget Hotel!

"No-no!" Walker shouted. He jumped to the side of the huge boulder and pushed.

The boulder ignored him and continued on the route that would send it crashing into the hotel.

"Ach! Push it aside, lads!" the dwarf leader bellowed.

The dwarves scrambled madly, seemingly in all directions at the same time, miraculously not bumping into each other or tripping one over the other. In seconds, they were at the side of the boulder, pushing. In a moment, they altered its track enough that it headed for the edge of the ridge and tumbled over on a trajectory that would take it wide of the Glittering Nugget.

Brushing his hands after looking to assure himself the boulder would miss the hotel, the chief dwarf said to Walker and Miss Kitty. "No need for an investigation."

"No need," Miss Kitty said.

"None, indeed," Walker agreed.

In a trice, the dwarves all vanished, carrying their casualties with them.

"Well," Walker said, wondering where the dwarves had disappeared to and how they had so quickly vanished. "I think now we can safely return to the hotel."

"Yes, before our erstwhile picnic companions start inventing reasons for our absence," Miss Kitty said.

Partway down the hill, during which they didn't speak of what had just happened, she suddenly said, "Some would say that where you put your hand was inappropriate."

"But you needed to go higher, and that was the most expedient way to boost you."

"Um hum. And in another time and another place..." Miss Kitty Belle picked up her pace and walked with a sway to her hips that hadn't been there before.

Smiling, Cheyenne Walker slowed down, and enjoyed the view.

T'AIN'T PROPER GRASS 'ROUND THESE HERE PARTS

"THAR THEY GO!" MAD COW BRAZOS SHOUTED, POINTING AT A cloud of dust halfway to the right.

"How'd they get over thar when they was jist a goin' thit away?" Rybekka Ramrodder, boss of the posse pursuing the bandits who'd just robbed the Fat Chance Saloon, shouted back, pointing at the edge of a bluff that stood slightly to the left of straight ahead.

"Danged if'n Ah knows," Brazos shouted, "but thit's gotter be them. Thit's the onlyst dust cloud in sight!"

"Now hold on thar," Ramrodder snarled, reining his horse to an abrupt stop, raising its own dust cloud.

The rest of the cow-pokers, card-barracudas, and back-shooters who made up the posse likewise reined in their cayuses, and gathered around Ramrodder, coughing to beat a drum and bugle corps from the dust they inhaled.

"If'n they was a goin' thit away, how'd they git over thar?" Ramrodder demanded, pointing first just left of straight ahead, and then halfway to the right.

A chorus of mumbles answered him. Except for one voice that spoke loudly and in the clear.

"Ah don't know how, but thit's gotter be them!" Hung Dawg Hooligan insisted, agreeing with his close friend Mad Cow Brazos.

Frustrated, Ramrodder glared around at the members of the posse, wondering if any of them were worth jack as trackers. His eyes instantly locked on Bozhonana, cousin of the late Zinni Injun Wathahiya, who had been the most excellent tracker the posse boss had ever known.

"You, Injun!" Ramrodder bellowed. "How'd they do thit? Go from thar to thar?"

Bozhonana didn't reply immediately. Instead, he leaned low over his cayuse's withers and stared blankly at the rocky ground, which had never taken a print—hoof, foot, or paw. After a long minute by Ramrodder's railroad watch, he lifted his head to look at the edge of the bluff slightly to the left of straight ahead, before swiveling to the rapidly disappearing dust cloud halfway to the right. Wordlessly, he pointed to where the outlaws had been seen disappearing around the bluff, then swung his arm halfway to the right.

Ramrodder gave him a hard stare, working his jaw like he actually had a plug of tobacco in his cheek, knowing full well he'd quit chawing two days before. Abruptly, he nodded decisively, and declaimed, "They went thit away!" But before he could spur his cayuse in pursuit of the no-longer-visible dust cloud halfway to the right, Pettigrew Sasparella, owner of the recently robbed Fat Chance Saloon, objected strenuously.

"S'not possible fer them ta be thar an' then thar," he declared, while pointing in the usual directions. "It were mah saloon what wuz robbed, an' Ah'm goin' after 'em whar they was seen. Who's a'comin' with me?"

Once more there was a chorus of mumbles as the other members of the posse considered the options. On the one hand there was the direction where the outlaws had last been seen. On the other was the mysterious dust cloud that had come out of nowhere, and just then gone back to nowhere.

Sasparella didn't wait to hear who might join him, he just spurred his cayuse into a gallop slightly to the left of straight ahead.

Ramrodder, relying on the ambiguously wordless direction given by Bozhonana, shouted a rousing, "Foller me!" and galloped off halfway to the right, toward where he'd last seen the dust cloud.

⚊⚊⚊◄◆►⚊⚊⚊

Three miles farther on, with the dust cloud clearly in sight once more and rapidly growing, and his cayuse lathered something fierce, Ramrodder reined in to a walk, and looked back to see how close his posse was. The dust cloud was too dense for him to tell, but it didn't look big enough to hide all eighteen of the posse's members. Soon enough, the rump posse caught up and the dust settled enough for him to count his trailers. He almost heaved a sigh of relief when he saw Bozhonana amongst them.

"Tarnation!" Ramrodder swore, when he saw only half of the expected riders gathering around. He looked to the distance and saw a rapidly shrinking dust cloud where the other half of the posse vanished around the edge of the distant butte. "How's we gonner round up alla them thieving thieves 'thout the whole posse?"

Skunk Beansworth took a deep breath and ventured, "If'n Bozhonana wuz right, we gwine meet up with t'others right soon now."

"When was that Injun ever right?" Polecat Asskroft demanded.

But Rybekka Ramrodder paid him no more mind than he'd given Skunk Beansworth; he'd put spurs to his cayuse and soon was closing to rock-throwing range of the fleeing dust cloud. The clattering of clopping hooves behind him said his truncated posse was doing its best to keep up. And maybe pass him.

Of a sudden, a wavering, like a wave of heated air springing off a baked flat rock, shot up in front of the dust cloud that Rybekka Ramrodder was now almost close enough to touch. In an instant, the pursued and presumed robbers of the Fat Chance Saloon vanished into it.

Not one to be thrown off even by something so unexpected, Ramrodder leaned forward over his horse's neck, thrust his Colt Junior Cadet six-shooter ahead like a cavalryman aiming his saber, gave full voice to a cry of, "CHARGE!," and plunged into the wavering air, into, into…

"Ah, Mista Ramrodder, suh," Scorpion Stung Shaunessey said in a most quavery voice as he hauled back on his cayuse's reins to haul it to a stop next to Ramrodder once they'd both passed through the shimmer in the air, "Ah don't think we's in Arizona no more."

"What in tarnation is thit?" Ramrodder blurted, not noticing the yelping and cursing of the remaining cow-pokers, card-barracudas, and back-shooters of his posse as they yanked and jerked on their reins, to avoid crashing into Ramrodder and Shaunessey, and anybody else who had made it through the shimmer in the air before they did. Not even when Sidewinder Calhoun's mount tumbled to its knees and threw the cow-poker teakettle over spurs face-first into the ground cover.

What Rybekka Ramrodder saw was a buckboard. But a buckboard unlike any buckboard the posse boss had ever before seen. It was twice the width of a Conestoga wagon, and taller than a Butterfield Overland Stage Company stagecoach. The bulk of the vehicle blocked him from a view of its front end, so he couldn't see the horses that were pulling it—had to be pulling it. Even so, he should have heard the *cloppity-clop* of their hooves. What he heard instead was a rumble like the purring of the giantest cougar anybody ever heard of.

Only then did Ramrodder notice that the buckboard wasn't raising a concealing cloud of dust, and wondered why not. He looked down and didn't see the dirt-and-gravel-and-flat-rock ground over which the posse'd been pursuing the conveyance, or even wheels underneath the buckboard. Instead, the ground was densely covered in fat, succulent-like leaves. What was more, the leaves were purple instead of a proper green! And the buckboard was hauling along a good foot and a half above the fat, purple leaves that were here and there overtopped by stalks that rose to man's height with branches out of their tops! Raven-like bird creatures perched on the branches, and eyed Ramrodder and Asskroft in a most hungry-like manner.

"Does ya think they's friendly?" Polecat Asskroft shouted, pointing to the side of the strangely huge buckboard.

Ramrodder looked where Asskroft pointed and briefly thought a passel of wild, screaming Injuns was galloping around the side of the buckboard. But that was only until he noticed that the blue feathers on their heads grew *out* of their heads instead of sticking up from a proper war bonnet. And their cayuses weren't horses, they looked like the ostriches from which plumes for ladies' hats came from, pictures of which Catastrophy Annie had shown him in *Godey's Lady's Book* once when he'd expressed wonder at the plumes. Another evidence that they weren't Injuns was they weren't *Redskins*, they had *Orange* skin. As final proof they weren't Injuns, Scalped Hunter's scalp, which always bled in the presence of Injuns, wasn't bleeding.

"They's armed!" Scalped Hunter screamed, cranking off a poorly aimed round from his Buntline Special. The reason his shot was poorly aimed was he was twisting out of the way of a projectile flung out from somewhere within the mob of Orangeskins.

The feather-headed Orangeskins screeched a horrendously loud warbling as they charged at the posse. Their mounts sped in high-stepping galumphs, which bounced the Orangeskins wildly up and down, and sidewise as well, so that Rybekka Ramrodder pondered how it was possible for them to retain their seating on their bipedal critters. They were each and all twirling an arm in circles over their heads, looking like nothing so much as so many army sergeants signaling their troops to "Rally 'round me, boys!"

"'They's slinging slings!" Skunk Beansworth suddenly cried out.

And verily, an Orangeskin would stop twirling his arm, and a hitherto unseen on account of its moving-so-fast pouch at the end of an equally previously-unseen-due-to-its speed-of-movement cord would send forth a projectile in the same manner as the biblical sling the shepherd boy-not-yet-King David used to kill the Philistine giant Goliath.

Fortunately, the jouncing of their rides prevented the Orangeskins aim from being anywhere near as accurate as that of the Savior of the Israelites, and all of their slung shots missed.

Also fortunate, was the speed of the high-stepping galumphs of the Orangeskins' mounts wasn't all forward, some of it was to one side or the other, which had them close slowly with the posse. That gave the cow-pokers, card-barracudas, and back-shooters time to steady their skittery cayuses, and even time enough for Sidewinder Calhoun to dust himself off and climb back into the saddle.

Ramrodder again chawed on the plug of tobacco he didn't have in his cheek, and gave the charging Orangemen an if-looks-could-kill look. "Skunk," he addressed Skunk Beansworth, "ya got yer Sharps loaded with yer holy-water bullets?"

"Yah, suh, the ones blest by the Holy Pope in Rome hisownself."

"I don't know if them Orangemen is devils or demons, or jist weird fellers. But yer holy water bullets might could be the onlyst things that kin hurt 'em.

Are you ready to do it?"

"Ah'm sure 'nuff ready," Beansworth answered, as his chest swelled with pride at the trust Rybekka Ramrodder placed in him.

"Polecat, Scorpion Stung," Ramrodder continued, "You got yer scatterguns ready?"

Polecat Asskroft broke open his three-barrel Remington shotgun to check that all three chambers were loaded. "Got one slug and two buckshots," he shouted, and pointed his triple muzzles in the general direction of the galumphing Orangemen.

"Double-ought buck!" Scorpion Stung Shaunessey confirmed, having checked the loads in his Winchester Model 1877 shotgun. He readied his aim.

Preparing to give the order to open fire on the Orangemen, Ramrodder leveled his Colt Junior Cadet at the mass of jinking and jiving Orangemen, knowing full well that it was hit or miss that he'd hit one of them because of their manic movement, when an Orangeman bigger than the others and whose feathers were longer and pink and turquoise instead of blue—he looked to be about the same size as a full-grown man—burst through the manic mob and flung his arms out to the sides. The creature twisted around on its long-legged, bulbous-bodied, long-necked mount and cawed out a cackling speech.

The attacking Orangemen reined in their galumphing mounts, faced the big one who appeared to be their chief, and looked to give him their full attention.

"Hold yer fire!" Ramrodder bellowed at his raggle-taggle rump posse. It was an order only obeyed by the three he'd given firing orders to—the others were too busy gawping at the powerful-strange Orangemen to have readied their weapons to fire on the presumed saloon robbers.

The pink-and-turquoise feathered Orangeman finished cackling at his Davidish slingers and turned to look directly at Rybekka Ramrodder and speak. His voice, surprisingly, wasn't a cackle but a rich and sonorous baritone, and his words and manner of speech weren't caws, but rather those of an Eastern Dandy. This neither surprised nor discomfited Rybekka Ramrodder. Having never met or even seen a tintype of an Eastern Dandy; for all he knew Eastern Dandies all had orange skin and grew pink and turquoise feathers out of their scalps.

"Mr. Ramrodder, might I inquire as to the purpose behind your band of obvious ruffians pursuing my hoverloader through the portal with such evident unfriendly intent?"

Ramrodder was briefly struck dumb by the sound of the words coming out of the mouth of this peculiar *person* who might be an Eastern Dandy. The delay was because he had to mentally translate the Orangeskin's accent into the sounds of normal folks' talk. He recovered rapidly enough, gave the plug of tobacco that wasn't there another chaw, realized the Dandy had addressed him by name. "Thit's my name, all right. Now what's yers?"

The Orangeman warbled a short series of sounds that could have been clicks, but just as easily might have been all soft vowels like the Navaho up around the Four Corners talked. He cocked his head. "That's my name in my language. However, your vocal apparatus can't manage those magnificent nomens. So, you may call me Fred."

"Well, Fred, we's a chasing you on account'a you robbed the Fat Chance Saloon. I'm hereby placing you and your passel of outlaws under arrest and taking y'all and that—that—whatever it was you called your buckboard—back to West Archaic, where you'll stand trial for robbery, and the money and other valuables you stole will be returned to them from which you stole 'em."

"Oh?" the boss Orangeman said languidly. "The Fat Chance Saloon, you say. Might you be referring to that ramshackle edifice filled with inebriates which I observed in West Archaic?"

Ramrodder chomped down hard on his not-there chaw, and muttered, "Good thing Pettigrew Sasparella didn't hear you describe his pride and joy in such negative terms." Although he had to admit to himself that the taverner might have too much difficulty translating the wordage of this here Eastern Dandy into normal folks' language to understand the monstrous slight just cast at the Fat Chance Saloon.

"And why on the eight planets of your solar system and the dozen of mine would we want to rob the Fat Chance Saloon? What could it conceivably harbor that I might have even the slightest possible interest in acquiring by any means, foul or other?"

Ramrodder sputtered, spraying saliva in all directions both to his sides and straight ahead. "What?" he roared when he sufficiently regained control of his vocal apparatus to tack one syllable onto the back of the preceding one for both to make sense. "What might the Fat Chance Saloon have worth stealing? Why the silver and copper coins with which the patrons of the Fat Chance Saloon pay for the booze they slosh down. Not to mention the occasional pinches of gold dust they pays with."

The pink-and-turquoise feathered Orangeman threw his head back and screeched out a laugh so loud and profane it startled into flight the raven-like birds which had resumed their ominous perches.

"How do you propose to accomplish this marvel—arresting us, I mean?" Fred's facial features shifted so that had he been human, Ramrodder would have thought he raised an eyebrow and curled his lip in a sneer. "Assuming, of course, that my band of servitors and I had the astonishingly bad taste to enter the Fat Chance Saloon, to rob it or for any other reason."

"We's a duly constituted posse, charged with bringing in the miscreants what robbed the Fat Chance Saloon. We's the posse, and you's the miscreants. Ah'm hereby placing y'all under arrest. So if'n yer men'll lay down their weapons, we'll escort you to Archaic and hand y'all over to Sheriff Shothip to deal with you proper like."

"Ah. So, Mr. Ramrodder, you aren't the sheriff?"

"No, I ain't. But we's a duly constituted posse, like I said."

Fred made a show of counting the posse, then turned his head as to assess the number of his followers. "Mr. Ramrodder, I dare say we've got you outnumbered by at least four to one. You can't arrest us unless we agree to being arrested. Which we don't."

"Ah, Mr. Ramrodder, suh," Skunk Beansworth stage whispered, "Fred do have a point."

Before the posse boss could frame a response to the Orangeman boss, the Orangeman spoke up. "As I said, you aren't the sheriff. Even if you were, you have no jurisdiction here."

Polecat Asscroft glanced around furtively and muttered, "Wharever here is." It didn't look like anyplace he'd ever seen, or even heard of, in the Arizona Territory.

Ramrodder spat out a long streamer that would have been brown if he'd actually been chewing on a plug of tobacco, and mulled over the situation. Fred was likely right about the posse not having jurisdiction wherever here was, and he was abso-posi-lutly right about the Orangemen greatly outnumbering the posse. But he and his men *were* charged with bringing in the robbers. So, one way or another, it had to be done.

"Well now, Fred, if'n you'll tell your, your..." for lack of a better word, "...men to lay down their slings, we'll escort you back to Archaic."

"I rather think not," Fred answered in a tone that suggested that he was looking down his nose at the posse boss. He raised his hand in what was probably the beginning of a signal to his befeathered force to resume charging and slinging, but was forestalled by a commotion to the rear of the posse.

Suddenly, there came a clatter of frightened or startled cayuses' screams, neighs, and whinnies, and the shouts, roars, and curses of startled or frightened cow-pokers, card-barracudas, and back-shooters to confuse and or startle everybody on both sides, and even set the bipedal mounts of the befeathered heathens to gallumping madly in place. There was also the clearly heard yipping of a hitherto unseen or at least unnoticed dog. Rybekka Ramrodder neither saw nor noticed the dog, but nonetheless was certain it was neither Rin Tin Tin nor Lassie.

Ramrodder stood in his stirrups and twisted about to see what the cause of the commotion was, and was greeted by the sight of Pettigrew Sasparella and the possemen who'd galloped off with him to slightly left of straight ahead, and a quartet of ruffinish rascals being pursued by the Sasparella half-posse bursting through the same waver in the air through which Ramrodder and his half-posse pursued the feathered characters and their improbable if not downright impossible buckboard.

The ruffians didn't stop or even pause when they crashed through the rear guard of the possemen already there, but roared through the front rank of the posse and slammed straight on into the mass of milling Orangemen, sending many of them tumbling and spinning like so many ninepins, and themselves tossing and turning from being thrown by their stumbling cayuses.

"Stop 'em!" Pettigrew Sasparella shrieked. "They's the robbers what robbed mah saloon!" He clumsily guided his galloping cayuse on a slalom run through Ramrodder's half of the posse, and managed not to dislodge anybody, least of all himself, from their saddles. Which is more than could be said about the possemen behind him, who did collide with the riders already on the scene, knocking several to the, the, ah, the purple succulent-like ground cover.

Fred skittered his bipedal mount sidewise to avoid any collision with the ruffians or Sasparella's possemen and only suffered a minor bump that skittered his mount in a different direction. Stretching his head high on his long neck, the Orangeman chieftain click-warbled something that it appeared his host understood, as they quickly steadied their galumphing critters, even the ones who'd had to remount after being knocked tumbling and spinning to the succulent ground cover.

Pettigrew Sasparella leapt off his cayuse onto the back of a ruffian who'd been flung groundward due to slamming into three of four of the Orangemen. "Get the rest o' them!" he shouted as his weight knocked the wind out of the one he'd landed on.

There was more milling and colliding as his rump possemen scrambled among the by-then-mostly-mounted Orangemen to reach and secure the remaining saloon robbers.

"Dang!" Sasparella swore, looking around once the quartet was properly trussed.

"Ain't none o' them little-bitty tree thangs high 'nuff fer a proper hanging!"

"Hold on thar, Pettigrew," Ramrodder shouted. "We ain't havin' no lynching. We's takin' them robbers back to Archaic fer a proper trial, then a hanging, all legal like."

Pettigrew Sasparella grumbled, but conceded, "'Tain't no trees t' string 'em up nohows, so we may's well take 'em back." Then he looked around for the first time, taking in the landscape, the improbable buckwagon, and finally the weird befeathered, ah, men and the longnecked critters they were mounted on.

"Whar is we, and what is them?" he demanded.

"Danged if'n I knows," Ramrodder said. "But thet Eastern Dandy with the fancy headdress growing out'n his head is called Fred and the rest o' them's his, ah, folks."

"Zat so?" Sasparella said, casting a cocked eye at Fred. To his part of the posse, he said, "Lash 'em t' their cayuses, an' les skeddale back t' Archaic. After," he suddenly remembered, "I gets back the money they done stolen from mah Fat Chance Saloon!" As an afterthought he added, "When we gets home, a free drink fer everybody what helped me catch these desperadoes."

There came a ragged cheer from the possemen, even the ones who'd stayed with Ramrodder instead of going with him in pursuit of the robbers. Sasparella shot a gimlet eye at them, but otherwise kept his peace.

"Fred," Ramrodder said loudly enough for everybody to hear, "Mah 'pologies to you and yourn fer the fully understandable misunderstanding. You're free to go about your business. We's goin' back t' Archaic fer a trial and hanging, right legal like."

"Oh? You and your band of ruffians detain me and my warriors and think you can dissmiss me in so cavalier a manner?"

Not being sure of what a "cavalier manner" was, Ramrodder gave a chaw and spat out a streamer that would have been brown if he hadn't given up chawing tobacco. "Wall now, you can do whatever you wants, but me and my posse are going home." So saying, he raised his arm and swung it around in a circle, like an army sergeant signaling "Rally 'round me, boys," and flung his hand toward the wavering in the air through which they could see the scrubby, rock-covered ground they expected to see in arid Arizona. He started herding his possemen and the captured outlaws back to familiar ground when a warbling caw made him twist back to see what the ruckus was.

It was Fred, his head high on his stretched neck singing at the sky, exhorting his Orangemen into action. Around and behind him his "warriors" took up the cry and urged their mounts into gallumphing movement, forward and back, side to side, twirling their arms above their heads so fast their hands were blurs. When they stopped twirling, rocks flew out from the slings they were slinging. Fortunately, nearly all of the rocks flew high or wide or in between cayuses and their riders.

"They's shooting at us again!" Ramrodder shouted, and drew his Colt Junior Cadet to fire an ill-aimed shot more-or-less in the direction of Fred, which shot went either high or wide. Whichever, it missed.

"Retreat!" he shrilled, and resumed herding his band of cow-pokers, card-barracudas, and back-shooters, but with great urgency. To his sides he heard the roar of shotguns, as Polecat Asscroft and Scorpion Stung Shaunessey, not having stood down, let rip with their statterguns. The blasts, being no better aimed than Ramrodder's shot, had no visible effect on the mass of Orangemen.

"Git out'n mah way!" Skunk Beansworth shouted at Scalped Hunter as the two crashed shoulders together on their way through the weird wavering in the air.

"After you," Mad Cow Brazos said to Hung Dawg Hooligan, Giving him a courtly half-bow wave to pass through the airy waver before him.

"No, you first," Hung Dawg Hooligan replied.

"But Ah insists," Brazos insisted.

"You no go, me go!" the Injun Bozhonana shouted as he forced his way between the two and passed through the wavery air to the hardpan beyond.

"Both of you, git!" Ramrodder shouted, coming hard behind them. He yanked his Stetson off of his head and whipped both Brozos' and Hooligan's cayuses' rumps, startling the beasts into forward motion, and back to Arizona.

Once through himself, Ramrodder looked back and saw the wavering in the air collapse on itself. He looked around enough to see that none of the Orangemen or their curious mounts made it through before the waver closed, and that all of his posseemen seemed to have gotten through before he did hisowneself, Not yet certain that the waver wouldn't reopen, he kept his posse and their prisoners at a gallop until their cayuses were lathered up something fierce and some mayhaps in danger of collapsing, before he called for them to slow to a walk.

Back in what he was pretty sure was Arizona, he called for Bozhoanna to take the lead and guide them back to West Archaic.

Bozhanna fought to the front of the posse and stood high on his saddle, looking to the front and sides, raised his arm high, pointed toward the mesa around which Pettigrew Sasparella had led half of the posse in pursuit of the bandits, and then slightly to the right of the opposite direction.

"This the way!" he shouted.

Ranrodder gave the Injun a hard look that asked if he was sure, but didn't ask the question. Simply nodded for him to lead the way.

Bozhanna led the way he'd chosen. His direction wasn't too far off, and it only took the posse and their prisoners three times longer to make their way home than it had taken them to get to the point where they'd split up in the first place.

Finally, back at the Fat Chance Saloon, Pettigrew Sasparella stood every member of the posse to one drink on the house. Except for Skunk Beansworth, who managed to get a second shot of redeye.

The four robbers were locked in the back room of Heavy Thumb Tromp's general store for two days before Sheriff Hipshot came to take them to Archaic for trial. Pettigrew Sasparella and most of the posse went with him, both to guard the prisoners and to see the trial and subsequent hanging.

Afterwhich life went back to normal in the wild and wooly town of West Archaic, Arizona Territory.

GLASS SHADES

"MR. WALKER, SIR?"

The man in the well-brushed frock coat looked up from his luncheon in the Placer's Poke restaurant to see a young man in an Eton jacket and brimless square cap.

"Yes, Jack?" gambling man Cheyenne Walker said with a nod.

"A Babbage clack for you, sir." The bellhop extended a silver tray with an envelope on it.

"Thank you." Walker took the envelope and dropped a silver dollar in its place. He waited for the bellhop to back away before using a small folding knife to slit the envelope open. It contained a single sheet of paper with a message delivered via the Glittering Nugget's Babbage Analytical Engine. It read:

Mr. Cheyenne Walker
c/o the Glittering Nugget Hotel
Colorado Territory

My Dear Mr. Walker,

Mr. Pinkerton has given me an assignment on which I would most assuredly appreciate your assistance. It is of a nature similar to the several assignments on which we have co-operated in the past, and I cannot imagine acquiring such aid from another soul. Kindly respond to me as to whether or not you can join with me in this endeavor at the Dragon Bones Hotel, Zapotec, New Mexico Territory where I will sojourn in a week's time.

[signed,] Miss Kitty Belle
The Pinkerton Agency

Walker folded the message and inserted it into an inner pocket of his coat before hastily finishing his meal. Sated, he made his way to the check in desk.

"Ah, Mr. Walker," the officious Mr. Reghaster greeted him. "How might I be of assistance?"

"You can first tell me when the next stagecoach to Denver will be here."

Reghaster looked startled. "The stagecoach to Denver? Are you considering leaving us, Mr. Walker?"

"I am that."

"A coach comes from Denver daily, and makes the return in the afternoon."

"I will be on it. If you will kindly give me a sheet of paper, I need to send a clack. While you are doing that, I will retire to my room to get my luggage, then return here to settle my accounts."

"The hotel will surely miss you," Reghaster said as he pushed a sheet of paper across the counter. "It's so seldom we see a gambler with your skill and ability tithe the hotel so richly from his winnings."

Walker ignored the clerk while he scribbled out a message to Kitty Belle assuring her that he would endeavor to meet her in a week's time.

"Oh, that *woman* Pinkerton," Reghaster said with a disapproving headshake when he saw to whom the message was addressed. "A woman Pinkerton agent indeed!" He headed for the steam-operated Babbage Analytical Engine that would send a message to the Dragon Bones Hotel in Zapotec, New Mexico.

But Walker didn't hear him; he was already striding toward the Otis lifting machine that would spirit him to his room on the hotel's tenth floor.

Cheyenne Walker's room was waiting for him when he arrived at the Dragon Bones Hotel on the morning of the sixth day after leaving the Glittering Nugget. Miss Kitty Belle hadn't yet arrived, but, "We expect her daily," the hotel's proprietor assured him. Walker wasn't put off by the vagueness of her arrival time; travel across the plains and into the desert Southwest didn't lend itself to railroad timetable efficiency, not even with landships.

With hours or perhaps days to wait, he took advantage of the time to avail himself of the hotel's bath and barber. Freshly cleaned and coiffed, he dressed, with his Buntline Special discretely hidden away under his frock coat, then headed for the bar, where he was able to order a sausage and bread plate—the Dragon Bones not having a restaurant. After eating, he went in search of a card game. Not that he had to look far—the hotel's lobby also served as its gaming room. And that's where Miss Kitty Belle found him when she arrived on the next day's coach.

Walker was sitting where he could see the front door, and immediately rose to his feet on her entrance.

"Miss Kitty Belle!" he announced to the world.

"Mr. Cheyenne Walker," she replied with a dip of her head. "I'm surprised you can make me out under all this travel dust." Indeed, her long coat, bonnet, and muffler were covered with the dust of the trail.

Walker shook his head. "Your beauty of character shines through. I doubt that any thickness of dust, dirt, or even mud could disguise you from my sight."

A slight smile quirked her lips. "You speak too grandly, sir. Now I must see to my room and make myself presentable so I can join you for dinner."

Zapotec at the time was not a destination for holidaymakers, mostly a waystation for travelers passing on their way to southern Arizona or parts of Sonora, Mexico. Most of the people who stopped for longer than a meal and a night's sleep were geologists searching for the stones that some believed were the bones of giant animals that had failed to make it onto Noah's Ark.

Zapotec did, however, boast a cantina, a fact Walker ascertained while waiting for Miss Kitty Belle to refresh herself. He entered and while he had a small beer—it was obviously a local brew—he examined the interior. Manny's cantina boasted six smallish tables, each with four chairs. The room was moderately clean—no rodents scampered about the floor—and the scents wafting from the kitchen suggested the food was on the good side of palatable. The only language he heard spoken by the few customers present was a doggerel mix of border-Spanish and one or more local Indian languages.

Satisfied, he returned to the Dragon Bones to await the Pinkerton agent. He didn't expect to have to wait long, as he knew that Kitty Belle was of a practical bent. He was right. In hardly more time than he would have expected to wait for a man to bathe and dress, she descended the stairs from the hotel's upper level.

"Miss Belle," he said as he stood from an otherwise unoccupied table. He looked with approval at her garb; a simple gingham dress, just short of ankle length, with sleeves that reached mid-forearm. A bonnet of the same material perched on her head

"Mr. Walker," she said brusquely. "You were right about the bathwater. Now, I am famished. Have you torn yourself away from the gaming tables long enough to find a place to eat away from prying ears?"

"I have," he assured her." He offered his arm and led her to the exit.

⟿•◖◗•⟿

They took a table next to an open window where they would garner the benefit of whatever refreshing breeze might pass their way. The young senorita who took their food and drink order tittered at Walker's hesitant Spanish, even though it was better than her broken English.

Cheyenne Walker positively beamed at Miss Kitty Belle while they waited for their dinner to be served. "It is such a delight to see you again, Miss Belle. The three times in the past when I have joined with you on your detectiving were marvelous exercises. I look forward to this one, even though I have no idea what your mission is."

They paused when their food and drink were delivered, and then Kitty Belle broached the reason she wanted Walker with her on this assignment.

"Local lawmen, both town marshals and county sheriffs," she began after tasting the stew and nodding approval of the dish, "have of late been assiduous about bringing law-breakers to justice. Three are serving lengthy prison terms for bank robbery, one is waiting the gallows for the murder of a coachman in commission of a robbery, and several others are either in jail for short sentences or have fled to distant parts.

"But," she said, waving her spoon about like a conductor's baton, "then there is the matter of the Hannity gang. Four of the five members of the gang were killed when they chose to fight a posse rather than surrender when they were caught. They are the gang leader Bloodstained Ralph Hannity, Lonesome Georgie Throckton,

Hammerhands Sue Blackson, and a Zinni Indian only known as Scalptaker."

"So, what is it about the matter of the Hannity gang that has aroused the interest of Mr. Pinkerton?" Walker asked when Miss Kitty paused to spoon more stew.

"As I said," she resumed, "four of the five members of the Hannity gang were killed fighting the posse. The fifth is incarcerated in the territorial penitentiary in Santa Fe."

Walker put his spoon down and spread his hands questioningly.

Miss Kitty Belle bestowed a small smile on Cheyenne Walker. "Mr. Pinkerton's attention has been aroused because it appears that the gang is still active."

Walker leaned back from the table. "An Indian is a member of the gang? Is Hammerhands Sue then a woman, like Calamity Jane perchance?"

She shook her head, causing her locks to bob about. "He uses his hammer-like hands to bring low anyone who laughs at his name."

Walker nodded, accepting her explanation, then mused, "Four are dead and the fifth is imprisoned. It's not possible for them to still be engaged in banditry."

"Now do you understand how this attracted Mr. Pinkerton's attention?"

"I do indeed."

"Now that we have eaten," she said, "we must hie to the town marshal and learn what we can about these supernatural banditries from him. Then to the newspaper office." She looked about for the young senorita and signaled her to join them. Miss Kitty Belle then surprised Cheyenne Walker by speaking in rapid-fire Spanish. The girl giggled as she scampered to the kitchen.

"I told her how delicious the stew was," she explained, acting on the assumption that Walker hadn't been able to follow her Spanish.

"So, I gathered," he said dourly. "To the town marshal then." He stood and pulled her chair out for her.

Had either of them bothered to look out of the window and down at the ground below it, they would have seen sitting against the wall a wizened old man wearing leggings, a breechcloth, a baggy shirt, and a reservation hat. A pristine golden eagle's feather stood up from the hat's brim. The old man eased himself from below the window before rising to his feet and ambling off.

Zapotec's town marshal had a tiny office in the municipal building. A slightly larger space was allotted to the town administrator and council. The largest of the building's three spaces had a wall of bars—the jail. Marshal Tom Peron was the town's only full-time employee.

After briefly identifying herself and Cheyenne Walker and their mission, Miss Kitty Belle said, "I'd like to question everybody who was on that stagecoach. Where can I find them?"

Marshal Peron scratched his chin in a thoughtful manner before saying, "You'll have t' talk ta One-Hand Krysler t' find out where they's gone. Ya know, they all lit out on the next stage after the robbery. 'Cept fer Mr. Jim D. Andy, who got kilt by the bandits and is now residing in our own Boot Hill. Doubt he'd be able to tell you much, though."

"And where might One-Hand Krysler be?" Kitty Belle said, dismissing Mr. Andy as a possible source of information.

"Par'bly somewheres 'tween here and Aztec City. Don't rightly know when he might be back in these parts again', on account'a because he was talkin' 'bout quittin' the stage drivin' business after getting' robbed by mechanicals what shot and kilt one a his payin' passengers." The marshal stopped talking for a moment while he pensively scratched at the stubble on his chin. "That might have had sumpin to do with him quittin' stage drivin'."

"Mechanical men?" Cheyenne Walker and Kitty Belle exclaimed simultaneously.

"Thas what One-Eye said."

"What did the passengers say?" Miss Kitty asked.

Peron shook his head. "They was all in too fired a hurry to git outta town to say anything. 'Cept, o' course, fer that Mr. Andy, what weren't in no hurry to go nowheres nohow. 'Course others as witnessed the robbery still claims it'twere the Hannity Gang, though they's mostly dead."

Miss Kitty made a moue at the unhelpful news. "All right, do you at least have pictures of the supposed highwaymen?"

"That I do!"

Marshal Peron's pay was little enough that he found it necessary to supplement it in various ways. One of which was to charge admission to the jail for the curious to see captured miscreants. Another was...

"Yep, Ah has pitchers of the Hannity Gang when their bodies was brung in," he said. "We stood 'em up right nice again' the wall of the 'nicipal building." He pointed to the right of the entrance. "We took pitchers of each of 'em and a pitcher of all of 'em."

"Wonderful. I'd like copies of each of the pictures."

"Thas right kindly of you, Missy. Since youse buyin' all of 'em, I'll give you a cut price; all of the singles fer thirty cents 'stead of ten cents each, and thirty cents fer the four of 'em together. Why I'll even throw in a pitcher of Lefty Lazlow what's in prison fer free, seein' how youse a lawman, ah, I means a law *lady* yersef."

"Marshal Peron," she gasped. "Why, that's robbery."

He shook his head. "I know Mr. Pinkerton sent you here to investigate, but Mr. Pinkerton don't pay me to take them pitchers. You want 'em, you gotta pay fer 'em."

"You want sixty cents for five photographs, and another one for free. Is that right?"

"Yes'm. That'll 'bout do it."

"Do you take the pictures yourself, Marshal?" Walker asked.

"Nossuh. The photography man is Wendell Kleghorn."

"And where might Mr. Kleghorn be?"

Peron waved a hand, indicating nowhere in particular. "Out there somewheres. Par'bly sellin' pitchers his ownself." He screwed up an eye to peer sharply at Walker. "Don' think you can get 'em fer nothing from him. He'd charge full price fer alla them, and wouldn't give you the Lefty Lazlow fer free, neither. He'd make you pay ten cents fer it."

"I'd expect nothing less. Photographing is a hard way to make a living. How do you come by your copies?"

"Ever time Wendell come through here, he prints out new 'uns fer me. I gives him half the money I got from sellin' the las' bunch."

"Does Mr. Kleghorn carry the glass plates with him?"

"Nossuh!" They's too val'able fer that. They's locked up in the bank vault."

"Mr. Kleghorn seems to be a very wise businessman."

Peron started to reply, but Miss Kitty cut him off. "Marshal, I would very much like to see a place where people reported the Hannity Gang committing banditry after they were killed or incarcerated."

Peron *harrumphe*d at the interruption and muttered something about Kleghorn being very wise, then talked.

"Don't know what you think you kin find. Las' week they robbed a stage a few miles from here. If'n it were the ghosts of the Hannitys, there ain't nothing to find no how. Not even if they's mechanical men, like One-Eye Krysler said. If'n it were other highwaymen, they's likely long gone from these parts. Either way, you're wasting your time."

"What do you mean, by mechanical men?" Kitty Belle asked.

Peron shrugged. "Thas what ole One-Eye said. 'Course he stunk of whiskey when he said it, so who knows."

"And those passengers?" Walker asked. "What did they say?"

Peron shook his head. "They was too scart to say nothing. They jis wanted t' move on as fast as they could." He shook his head again. "Don't think you'll find nothin'"

"When Mr. Pinkerton tells me to investigate something, I do it, no matter how unlikely it is I will find anything. So, where do we go?"

Peron shrugged. "Take the south road till it turns east, then go..."

"Now the newspaper office?" Walker suggested when they left the municipal office.

"Indeed. The newspaperman might know something more."

But the office of the *Zapotec Herald* was closed.

⟶◦◎◦⟵

Two hours later and five miles southeast of Zapotec, Walker pulled back on the reins to stop the horse drawing their hansom carriage.

"That doesn't look much like the tree Marshal Peron described," Kitty Belle said of the tree next to which they'd stopped.

"But it is the only tree within two miles in either direction," Walker observed.

"And there does seem to be trace of a wagon stopping and something happening to the side of the road," Kitty Belle added. "Let us look more closely."

Before leaving Zapotec they had changed their garb. Walker doffed his frock coat and ruffled shirt in favor of a denim shirt. Kitty

Belle had changed from her gingham dress to denim culottes and waistshirt.

Before stepping down from the hansom, Walker took his Buntline Special in its belted holster from the satchel he'd carried them in. He donned the belt as soon as his feet were on the ground, and immediately reached up to help Miss Kitty dismount. She didn't need the assistance. Her Colt Peacemaker remained in its satchel, but the carrier was unlatched and in her hand.

This was a landscape of Fairy Dusters and Jacob's staff, dry awaiting the next rainfall. There were two sets of wheels. One was obviously from the stagecoach. The other showed that a wagon had angled across the road to block passage. An area of some square yards on the north side of the road had been smashed flat.

They stepped carefully through the Fairy Dusters around the smashed-down area and looked carefully into it and at the ground between the plants. When their circumnavigation led them back to the road, they spent a moment in thought before discussing what they'd just seen.

"The horses were cut loose and sent on their way, then the coach was toppled onto its side," Kitty Belle said.

Walker nodded agreement. "The hoof prints around the fallen coach are far too small to be the prints of dray horses."

"The footprints in the trampled area are obviously those of the men who righted the coach. There," she pointed at well-defined set of hoof prints on the road, "is where the new team was attached to draw the coach away."

Another set of footprints showed where the driver, his shotgun guard, and the surviving passengers had begun their trek to Zapotec.

Walker squatted in the road to examine other footprints that led from where the blocking wagon had stood to the coach. What he saw made him grimace. "These are far deeper than the other prints. Could it be that One-Eye Krysler was right about mechanical men?"

Kitty Belle didn't answer, instead looking east, away from Zapotec, toward some low mountains in the middle distance. After a moment, she said, "According to Marshal Peron, the only thing missing from the coach's cargo was the Wells Fargo strongbox. It's odd that the robbers didn't take the passengers' valuables from their persons."

"Unusual, indeed," Walker said. "I've never before heard of high-waymen leaving passengers with their valuables untouched." He looked back in the direction of town, and saw, faint with distance, the figure of a standing man, with what might be a feather sticking up from his hat.

With nothing more to be found at the site of the robbery, they got back into the carriage to drive back to Zapotec. When Walker got the rig turned about, the faintly seen man was nowhere in sight.

"Maybe the newspaper office will be open this time," Belle said.

⋘⟡⋙

Cheyenne Walker and Miss Kitty Belle heard the *klickety-klatter* of the newspaper's hand-cranked printing press before they reached the office of the *Zapotec Herald*. The noise, they discovered on entering through the unlocked door, was far greater inside than out. A man, closer in age to sunset than sunrise, stood at a printing press furiously cranking its handle as it spat out broadsheet after broadsheet. Between the noise of the press and the mufflers he wore over his ears, the man didn't hear them enter. It wasn't until Walker stepped to the printer and lifted a just-printed page that the man noticed his visitors. He pulled back the sheet feeder and continued cranking until the paper currently going through the machine cleared the mechanism.

He took off his ear-mufflers and wiped his hands on an ink-stained cloth.

"Maxwell Kirkpatrick, at your service," he said in too loud a voice. "Publisher, editor, reporter, and," with a wave at the press, "chief mechanic of the premier newspaper of Zapotec and surrounding territory. And you," his gaze swept up and down his visitors, "must be Miss Kitty Belle of the Pinkerton Agency, and her sometime companion-in-arms Mr. Cheyenne Walker!"

"We are," Kitty Belle said. "How did you guess?"

Kirkpatrick shook his head. "Guessing's got nothing to do with it. Among other things, I'm the top investigating reporter in this part of New Mexico Territory. Between that and being the publisher of the paper, it's my business to know who's stopping by. And," he raised a quizzical eyebrow at Walker, "might you be carrying your Buntline Special?"

Walker raised an equally quizzical eyebrow at the question. "It's in my room at the hotel."

"Dime-novelist Ned Buntline had only commissioned half a dozen of the Colt Army revolvers with 12-inch barrels, which he gave to top lawmen. I don't expect you'll tell me how you came by yours?" He turned to Kitty Belle and asked, "And you have your Colt Peacemaker?" That .45 caliber pistol was often preferred by lawmen.

"I do," she replied. Then, "We came to see you this morning, but the office was closed."

"Of course, it was. I was up in the hills interviewing some of the geologists who are digging up the dragon bones buried there." He continued talking more loudly than necessary.

"Dragon bones," Walker said. "Surely you don't believe they are finding the bones of real dragons that didn't make it onto Noah's Ark."

"Course not. That might be what the unlettered denizens of this region might think, but not everybody does. The name caught on, though. Anyway, it's easier to call them that than to use that made-up name, *dino-saurs*.

"But you aren't here to find out about the dragon bones, you're investigating the reports that the deceased members of the Hannity gang are still committing robbery."

"Yes, we are," Kitty Belle said. "All of the witnesses are long gone. We hope you might have interviewed them before they left town, and can give us information."

"I did, and I wrote it up in the paper each time the mysterious robbers—be they mechanical or spectral—victimized folks. I don't imagine you've had opportunity to read my stories. Most people hereabouts use the paper in the outhouse, even if they don't read it first." He shook his head sadly. "But! I have archive copies, and you're more than welcome to sit yourselves down and read them while I continue printing out the new edition."

"Do you mind if we take them somewhere else to read?" Kitty Belle gestured at the printing press.

"What? Oh, yes. Of course. I'm so used to the noise of the press I hardly notice it anymore." He went to a cabinet and shuffled through stacks of broadsides, occasionally pulling one out. When he'd assembled half a dozen, he handed them to Walker.

"Kindly remember to return them after reading," Kirkpatrick said to Kitty Belle, still at high volume.

"We surely will," she said with a smile. She gave him half a bob as she turned to leave the newspaper office.

"One more thing," Walker said before following her. "What can you tell us about Mr. Kleghorn's background, has he always been an itinerant photography man?"

Kirkpatrick paused as in thought, then said, "Don't know if it's true, but there's a story that Wells Fargo foreclosed on his family farm back in Iowa. Could be true. Could be not." He shrugged.

"Thank you, Mr. Kirkpatrick." Walker exited and joined Miss Kitty on the boardwalk. They'd hardly gone a few yards before the *klickety-klatter* of the hand-cranked press took up again.

At Manny's Cantina, it being late in the afternoon, they sat at the same window-table as the day before, and ordered the beef stew over rice and a small beer before looking at the broadsheets. It was a simple paper, just one sheet printed on both sides.

"Priced at one penny," Walker noted.

Their reading disclosed that there had been six instances since the Hannity Gang's demise. Four were stagecoach holdups out on the road, two were in Zapotec when the coach was stopped to let off geologists. In each case, the only thing taken was the Wells Fargo strongbox. The box was always found along the road at a later time, broken open, its lock shattered, and contents missing. During the two robberies in town, the bandits had fired enough bullets to keep everybody ducking for cover and not shooting back.

Walker and Belle stopped reading when their stew arrived. After, when the bowls had been taken away and their small beers replenished, they resumed reading and discussing what they read.

"There doesn't seem to be a pattern to when or where they rob the stagecoaches," Miss Kitty said when she finished reading the last of the stories.

"None that I could discern either," Walker said. "Random times and intervals."

"Random places as well."

"But it's most interesting that rumor says Kleghorn's family farm was foreclosed by Wells Fargo, and the only thing stolen from the stagecoaches was the Wells Fargo strongbox," Walker said. "And I do note one other little piece of coincidence."

Kitty Belle shot him a look. "And what might that be?"

"The two times the Hannity Gang robbed in Zapotec, Mr. Kleghorn was here in town."

"I, too, saw that coincidence."

They sat in silent contemplation for a few minutes when something indistinct caught Walker's attention. He stood and stuck his head out of the window. Looking down he saw crouching a wizened old man in leggings, breechcloth, and baggy shirt. A golden eagle's feather stuck up out of the hatband of his reservation hat. The man grinned at him before scuttling away.

"What has your attention?" Miss Kitty asked.

"An old Indian. He brings to mind a figure I faintly saw after we examined the site of the latest robbery."

It being past dusk now, they returned to the Dragon Bones Hotel. Miss Kitty Belle retired to her room to await sleep and dawn, when they might head into the badlands in search of any geologists who might shed light on the robberies.

For his part, Walker went to the lobby-gaming room, where he was careful to not win too much from any one person.

The next morning, after a hearty breakfast of eggs, shredded pork, and potatoes with several cups of coffee, Cheyenne Walker was in the livery stable seeing to the lease of two horses for the day, when a clatter of hooves and excited shouting from the street drew his attention. He stepped to the stable doors to see what the noise was about—a stagecoach was pulling up and raising a cloud of dust.

"It's the Hannitys!" the driver shouted, jumping down from his driving bench. "Everbody out!" he screamed as he sped from the coach.

The shotgun guard had dropped down from his place and yanked the cab door open to let the passengers out; a man and two women stumbled onto the street and followed the guard as he headed for the nearest doorway.

Just then four fiercely bellowing horsemen, pistols drawn and firing into the air, surrounded the abandoned coach, sending the lathered horses bucking and screaming, in a panic to break free from their traces and flee from the bandits.

Walker spun about and, in three rapid strides, was at his valise, opening it and yanking out his Buntline Special. Before he got back to the door, he heard the powerful blast of a Colt Peacemaker from the direction of the hotel. Sure enough, when he looked, he saw Kitty Belle in the window of her room, raining bullets down on the bandits. Walker wasted no time adding his .45 caliber bullets to those fired by the Pinkerton agent.

To no evident avail. None of the quartet seemed in the least discommoded by being so shot at!

"It's the Hannitys," someone shouted, and was echoed by other voices.

Shouting and laughing, one leapt onto the coach and pulled the Wells Fargo strongbox from its place under the driver's bench and held it over his head like a trophy. He leaped directly into the saddle of his mount, and the four lit out so fast Walker could hardly tell into which direction they disappeared.

Marshal Peron appeared from the doorway of the municipal building with a shotgun, its double-barrels still smoking in his hands.

"Marshal!" Walker shouted, reloading. "I will join your posse to go after them."

"As will I," Miss Kitty cried as she spun about to leave her room.

Peron sadly shook his head. "Ah cain't raise a posse. Ma jurs'diction ends at the town line."

But neither Walker nor Kitty Belle heard him; Walker had run back into the stable to saddle the two horses he'd been preparing to lease, and the Pinkerton agent was pounding down the stairs to the ground floor while the Marshal said he couldn't raise a posse.

Walker led the two saddled horses out and was mounting up when Miss Kitty joined him and leapt on the other horse. Only then did they notice the town marshal standing in the doorway of the municipal building and that the other armed men who had also shot at the gang were just standing about.

"Well, Marshal," Walker shouted, "get the posse together and let's go after them."

Peron shook his head again. "Like Ah said, Ah cain't. Ma jurs'diction ends at the town line."

Miss Kitty Belle glowered at him, then stood in her stirrups and shouted out, "I am an agent of the Pinkerton Detective Agency, *my* jurisdiction goes beyond the town line. Who amongst you will join my posse?"

There was some hemming and hawing among the armed men, then half a dozen of them grudgingly agreed to join up.

While Walker and Belle waited for them to get their horses, they examined the ground around the stagecoach.

"I know I hit at least two of them," Kitty Belle muttered.

"As did I," Walker murmured. "Then why isn't there any blood in the street?"

"And why did I hear what sounded like bullets striking iron?"

The old Indian Walker had seen scuttling away from Manny's Cantina suddenly appeared between them.

"They be spirits *inside* metal men," he intoned. "Mortal bullets cannot harm them. The picture man has stolen their souls. You will not find them. Only ancient magic can put an end to this."

"We have to try," Kitty Belle answered him. Then to Walker, "Which way did they go?"

"I think west."

She looked at him. "You *think*?"

He shrugged. "They moved so fast I couldn't tell for sure."

Then the six men who volunteered for the posse arrived, joined by Marshal Peron.

"Ah cain't raise a posse. Don't mean Ah cain't *join* one."

Kitty Belle stood in her stirrups again and shouted, "Let's go!' she dropped into her saddle and led the way west. The Indian had disappeared. On the way out of town, the posse passed a wagon with fancy lettering on its side, proclaiming it to be the Photo-Graphy studio of Wendell Kleghorn. A twenty-foot pole holding an array of parabolic mirrors jutted from its roof, and its street-side panel was dropped down to display a collection of photographs for sale.

It was going on sundown when the posse returned to Zapotec. They were all dirty and sweaty and tired. All day long they'd searched without success to find any sign of the stagecoach robbers.

The hotel's bath had fresh water. Miss Kitty Belle bathed first, and the water wasn't too muddy when Cheyenne Walker took his turn. When they were both bathed and dressed in clean clothes, they met in the lobby and decided to return to Manny's Cantina for dinner.

The young senorita still giggled at Miss Kitty's rapid Spanish, but politely curtsied and promptly brought them roast chicken with black beans and rice, and a small beer, along with a large cup of freshly boiled water that had been off the fire long enough to cool down.

They were too tired and hungry to talk immediately, but drank the boiled water and asked for more before touching the beer, which they drank while eating.

"So, Mr. Kleghorn was back in town at the same time as bandits appeared to purloin the Wells Fargo strongbox," Walker said halfway through eating his portion of chicken.

Kitty Belle nodded. "I do believe it is incumbent on us to talk to the photography man."

Walker nodded agreement, but was too tired to talk.

After eating they had another small beer.

Kitty Belle casually swept her gaze around the other tables, three of which were occupied by locals digging into their food with gusto and giving no indication that they were aware of the presence of the two gringos. Assured that no one was listening to them, she said in a low voice, "I am brought to mind of that old Indian who spoke to us whilst the posse was assembling." When she saw that Walker was absorbing her words she continued, "You are aware of the belief held by some Original Peoples of the American West that photographs steal souls, as he said?"

"Indeed. I have even read that Doctor Livingstone has reported such beliefs from darkest Africa."

"If such beliefs can be thought true, then it is possible that someone has stolen the souls of a notorious gang of miscreants and has them posthumously continuing their lives of crime."

Walker blinked at that, and looked into a space only he could see. After a moment he began to pensively murmur. "We have dealt with gremlins, Coyote and Raven, rock trolls and dwarves." He shook his head sharply. "That given, I do not find stolen souls to be totally preposterous."

She gave him a small smile. "My thoughts precisely."

"So, we must find whoever is stealing the souls..."

"And discover how he is using them to enrich himself."

"And finally put those souls to rest..."

"...In whatever Hades they are properly consigned to."

"And the person to start with is Mr. Kleghorn."

It was just as well that they were too tired to confront the photographer that evening, as he was ensconced in his room at the Dragon Bones Hotel, and had given the desk clerk strict orders that he was to be undisturbed before the next morn's breakfast.

In the morning, Miss Kitty responded immediately to Walker's knocking on her door.

"Kleghorn hasn't risen yet. So, we have time to break our fasts before talking to him," he said.

"Good. I'd rather speak to him on a full stomach than an empty one."

They again went to Manny's, where Manny's wife served them *huevos con carne*.

Back at the hotel they discovered that Winston Kleghorn had already departed.

"Heading west and then north into the badlands, I suspect," the desk clerk informed them.

At the livery stable they were able to lease the same horses they'd ridden the day before; riders and mounts were thus familiar with each other. Soon after discovering that they'd missed their quarry, they were mounted and headed west out of Zapotec. Two miles on, they saw the wagon tracks they'd been following turn north onto an ill-used trail. They followed them.

The land they traversed gradually changed from flat to gently rolling to more like a heaving sea. Arroyos began to appear between the heights. More than an hour after turning north, they saw a flashing in the near distance.

"I suspect that's sunlight sparking off the mirrors on the wagon's spire," Miss Kitty Belle said.

"I do believe you're right," Cheyenne Walker agreed. He stood in his stirrups to look ahead. When he sat again, he said, "Mr. Kleghorn has stopped his wagon. Unless he starts again, we should reach him in less than half an hour."

Walker was right in his estimation of when they caught up with the photography man's wagon. Four crudely-formed iron statues of men with glass plates in place of their heads stood alongside the wagon. A beam of light from the bottom mirrors of the spire was aimed at the back of each of the four statues, and a faint hiss of steam seemed to emit from them.

"If you are here to rob me," Kleghorn said when Walker hailed him from the wagon's left, "I put all of my money in the bank yesterday. I have nothing for you to take."

"No, Mr. Kleghorn," Kitty Belle said from the wagon's right, "we have no intention of robbing you."

The photographer jerked when he heard her and twisted. He peered sharply at her then said, "Ah ha! You're that Pinkerton who's come to investigate the robberies that some folks attribute to the Hannitys."

"You surmise correctly, Mr. Kleghorn. I am indeed that very Pinkerton agent. And I would have you answer some questions."

"Oh, you would, would you?" Kleghorn said, twisting about on the bench in attempt to keep both of his interlocutors in sight. "And what might be these questions you'd like answered?" He scrambled to the top of his wagon where, even though Walker was still on one side and Kitty Belle on the other, he felt less surrounded.

"Mr. Kleghorn," Kitty Belle said, "I could not help but make note of the fact that each of the times that the Hannitys committed a robbery in Zapotec, you were there as well."

"And we'd like to know where you were on the occasions when the gang struck elsewhere," Walker added.

"Maybe I will not tell you." As he said that, Kleghorn turned a crank on the spire, realigning the mirrors to focus their beams on the glass plates atop each of the metal men. Abruptly, the metal of the four flowed into the shapes of well-formed, fully clothed men bearing the familiar, if ghostly, features of the Hannity gang.

Kleghorn laughed wickedly and cackled at the quartet. "Kill them!" he shrieked, pointing at his antagonists.

Two of the Hannitys turned to Kitty Belle and moved in her direction. The other two did the same toward Walker.

Kitty Belle turned her horse about and galloped the short distance to Walker's side before spinning about to face the spectral bandits.

Walker drew his Buntline Special.

"Your bullets can't hurt them!" Kleghorn crowed.

Suddenly they heard the *DUM-da-da-dum-dum* of an approaching drum, and a keening singsong below the drumming.

Kleghorn looked in the direction of the sound, as did the resurrected Hannitys.

"What's that?" the photography man demanded of the air.

Walker and Miss Kitty glanced quickly at each other, both mouthed, "The old Indian?" They turned to look toward the approaching sound.

The drumming and keening grew louder. The old Indian appeared, walking up the side of the arroyo in which he'd been hidden until now. He stopped drumming when he reached the flat, and pointed his drumstick first at Scalptaker, then at the others one at a time. His keening turned into a different song.

"Kill that redskin!" Kleghorn shrilled at the bandits.

They ignored him, instead, after a long moment of listening, the four bandits reached up to their heads and pulled out the glass plates that jutted from beneath their shoulders. Abruptly, the four figures melted into naked, crudely formed mannequins, and a ghostly image arose from each of them to waft into the sky. The glass plates shattered into fragments glittering in the sun the apparitions rose out of them, and shortly vanished.

"You can't do that!" Kleghorn shrieked. "You are my creations!" He collapsed onto his hands and knees and wailed with his head hanging down. "All I wanted was to make Wells Fargo pay for stealing my family's farm." He raised his face to the sky. "Is that such a bad thing?"

Kitty Belle urged her horse to the side of the wagon, and she clambered to its roof.

"Mr. Winston Kleghorn, you are under arrest for robbery, and possibly for murder, as well."

Walker joined her. He knelt next to the photography man and quickly frisked him, checking for weapons. Kleghorn had a small pistol and a knife hidden in his coat, which Walker relieved him of. He used the knife to cut a strip from the photography man's shirt to bind his hands behind his back, then lifted the man and dropped him onto the bench of his wagon.

"Sir, I believe you have rid this territory of a menace," Walker said to the old Indian.

"They are now with the Great Spirit," the old man said. "What was done here was a great evil. Now those souls can rest." He turned to the arroyo from whence he'd come.

"Do you want to drive, or shall I?" Walker asked Miss Kitty when the Indian was gone from sight.

"I will drive," she said. Walker tied her horse's reins to the back of the wagon.

Back in Zapotec, they handed Kleghorn over to Marshal Peron, who dispatched a rider to the county seat in Aztec to inform them of the arrest and the remarkable events surrounding it.

The town council met briefly and decided to relieve the marshal of his duties until they could determine whether he knew about the magical glass plates. They then called a town meeting in the street in front of the municipal building to tell everybody what had happened.

They concluded with, "Somewhere out there are several Wells Fargo strongboxes. We are sure the bank will richly reward anybody who finds them."

"My job here is now done," Miss Kitty Belle said to Cheyenne Walker over a dinner of pulled pork with black beans at Manny's Cantina. "So, I will be on the next stagecoach east tomorrow. Are you going to stay and join the search for the strongboxes?"

"No. I don't hunt treasure. I make my way with cards. Maybe I'll try my luck in Aztec."

"Luck?" she asked with a twinkle in her eyes.

"...Is a lady," he said, smiling.

THE WITCH OF EL PASO

ERGEANT MALAKAI GRANT OF COMPANY L, NINTH CAVALRY, Buffalo Soldiers—freemen and freed slaves called such because of a perceived resemblance of their hair to the wool on the heads and shoulders of buffalo—called a halt next to a small stream. He sent two men upstream and two down as lookouts.

"Water your horses," he ordered. "Collect water to boil for ourselves later." He stood tall in his saddle and looked all around him in a sweep of the horizon. Not that he expected to see any hostiles, but he'd seen too much combat to neglect basic security measures. All he saw was what he expected to see in this southwestern-most corner of Texas; a couple of low mesas, ground cut through by dry arroyos, some agave, desert spoon, and false yucca, and the occasional cottonwood tree.

Satisfied that no threat approached, Grant dismounted and led his horse to the water. Just before his horse began to drink, Private Zebulon Jefferson galloped from upstream.

"Sarge," Jefferson shouted when he was close enough, "stop the watering. You gots to see what Sam an' me found upstream."

"What is it, Jefferson?"

"A body in the water. A colored."

"One of ours?" Grant asked.

"No, Sarge. Looks like he was a cowboy."

Grant shouted for the rest of the squad to mount up and assemble on him. As soon as the squad gathered, Grant ordered Jefferson to lead the way to where they had found the dead cowboy.

The corpse of a black man did indeed lay in the stream. The cowboy's neck was ripped out to the spine, dispelling any possible doubt that he was dead. Blood spattered the near bank of the small stream. Scuff marks on the ground showed where the cowboy had attempted to fight off his attacker.

"Squad, pair off!" Grant ordered once his men had a chance to look at the body. "Search the ground for two hundred yards in all directions from here. Look for tracks, or any sign of passage of whatever it was that did this horror. And," he asked looking at Jefferson, "where's his horse?"

Jefferson shook his head. "Don't know, Sarge. Weren't no horse round here when Sam and me found the cowboy. That's so, right, Sam?"

Private Sam Crockett bobbed his head. "That's right, Sarge. Only horses we seen here was ar' own."

"When we find that horse's tracks, we will follow them and kill whatever beast killed this cowboy. You have your orders. Now start searching,"

Dismounted, Grant stepped into the water and grabbed the cowboy's boots to drag the body onto dry ground. The body's clothes were tattered, as though ripped by an animal trying to get to the flesh within. Not only was his throat open to his spine, the creature had opened and hollowed out his gut into his rib cage. Only the meat of the arms and legs weren't chewed on. His leather chaps and elbow-length gloves didn't account for that—an animal strong enough to do the rest of the damage to this cowboy should have had no trouble gnawing them off. They did look like coyotes had gnawed on them.

Finished examining the corpse, Grant got a Mackintosh from his bedroll to wrap the body in for transit back to Fort Bliss, outside El Paso.

The only tracks the Buffalo Soldiers found were the hoof prints of a galloping horse. They followed them to where the horse had collapsed from exhaustion. Buzzards were feasting on the carcass. But there were no tracks of whatever the horse had run from.

⟞•❁•⟝

"Let me see him," Colonel John Harris said when Grant reported to him upon his squad's return to Fort Bliss.

"Yessir." Grant turned to face his squad. "Crockett, bring the remains here," he shouted.

Private Crockett dismounted and led his horse with its load to stand at attention in front of the Colonel.

"Lower him, carefully," Grant ordered.

"Yes, Sarge." Crockett undid the straps that held the Macintosh-wrapped body from behind his horse's saddle and carefully laid it on the ground.

Grant knelt next to it and opened the Macintosh to disclose the corpse.

Harris briefly looked, then signaled Grant to wrap it again. "Are you positive it's not one of ours?" he asked.

"Yessir. I know the face of every man in the company. He's not one of ours."

"In that case, he's not our concern. Take two men with you and convey that body to the sheriff in El Paso."

"Yessir. By your leave."

"Do it." Harris turned and marched back to his office.

"Crockett, Jefferson, you heard the colonel. Let's take him to the sheriff."

"Do we gotta do it now, Sarge?" Jefferson asked. "We ain't had dinner yet."

"Yes, we gotta do it now. I'll buy us dinner in town."

"I like that, Sarge," Crockett said with a wide grin. "That's sure to be better than whatever we'd get in the mess hall."

The Overland and Western stagecoach from New Mexico and points west rumbled to a stop in front of El Paso's Del Norte Hotel, where the driver and five of its six passengers debarked and made their way within. They immediately headed for the bar, where they basked in the cool air wafting from overhead fans and indulged in drinks chilled by cubes of ice. The shotgun rider clambered onto the roof of the coach where he unlashed a valise and small chest and handed them down to the remaining passenger.

"I believe these are yours, Mr. Walker," he said.

"Indeed, they are. Now if you will be so good as to carry the chest to the reception desk, you will have my gratitude." Cheyenne Walker, valise in hand, stood in the street for a moment looking at the mirrored towers rising above the hotel and several other buildings along the street, towers that glittered with the parabolic mirrors that focused sunlight to the below-ground boilers that provided the steam to power the various establishments along the throughfare before he mounted the plank sidewalk and entered the hotel.

"My name is Walker," he said to the desk clerk. "I Babbaged ahead to reserve a room."

"Yes sir, Mr. Walker. We were expecting you and I have your reservation right here." The man drew a partially filled-out form from the center drawer of his desk. "The Overland and Western may not have landships," he said in response to Walker's upraised eyebrow, "but it is an exceptionally reliable transportation firm.

"Now, if you will be so good as to sign here," the clerk indicated where on the form as he handed over a quill pen, "and deposit your surety, the bellman will gather your luggage and see you to your room. Will there be anything else?"

"I wish a bath and a shave, and my coat and hat require a good brushing after the dust of the road," Walker said as he signed and paid the surety.

"Of course, Mr. Walker. El Paso may be rustic around the edges, but you will find the Del Norte hotel has all of the amenities one expects of a grand hotel."

Later, refreshed from a bath in the hot water provided by the hotel's sun-powered boilers, and a shave by the hotel's barber, and with his hat brushed—in deference to the heat he left his freshly brushed coat in his room—Cheyenne Walker went out to discover the aspects of the city on the border. Not that there was much to be discovered. The short main street had the limited amenities to be expected of any Western town: A dry goods store, a butcher shop, a millinery store, a haberdasher, a law office next to the sheriff's office, three eateries, two bordellos, two gambling halls, and five drinking establishments, all in addition to the newspaper office. A livery stable, smithy, and an abattoir were located a short distance to the rear of the street.

The day being hot and sunny, there weren't many people about, just a few men in rolled-up shirt sleeves and sweat-stained hats. Walker greeted each of them amicably and was so greeted in return. Three or four women, clad in light colors with sleeves that only reached their elbows and hems that rose above their ankles, trod the boards. Three blue-clad cavalrymen, Buffalo Soldiers by the darkness of their skin, rode along the street, casually looking about. They didn't look at anyone or anything in particular, merely maintained the combat veteran's awareness of their surroundings so they could instantly react should danger appear.

After a time, feeling hungered, Walker entered the Longhorn Cafe where he had a steak and baked potato washed down with a cold beer. Later, he adjourned to The Holed Ace gambling salon for a turn at cards.

He saw a table of four Buffalo Soldiers playing poker. Some of the whites in the room shot unfriendly glances at the black soldiers. Walker went to their table.

"Gentlemen," he said. "Might I join you?"

One or two of them cast him a suspicious glance, but one said, "Sure. A white man's money is as good as a soldier's."

"Thank you." Walker took a seat and held out his hand to the soldier who said yes. "I'm Cheyenne Walker."

The soldier shook his hand. "Private Zebulon Jefferson." In a moment, all four of the Buffalo Soldiers introduced themselves and shook Walker's hand.

They played for a few hours, during which Walker was careful to not win any money. He did though, make sure Jefferson won a little bit from the others. Then, feeling a bit hungry again, he took his leave. Some unkind looks followed him as he strode through the gambling salon, but he paid them no mind. Maybe someday he'd come back and win some money from those who seemed to resent the Buffalo Soldiers.

Savory scents wafting from Falina's Cantina led him into what immediately became his favorite dining room.

It didn't take many more days for him to exhaust all the pleasures of El Paso and begin considering where to go next. Perhaps north into Indian Territory? Or mayhap farther east to the pleasure palaces of New Orleans? But he was in no hurry, and it would be another two days before a coach headed to Louisiana came through El Paso.

Once again, Cheyenne Walker was in Falina's Cantina enjoying a plate of pork burritos with refried beans and rice. He had selected a table that had his back to the wall, and from which he could see the entrance and all the windows. That was how he was immediately able to spot the ivory-complexioned woman in a not-quite-ankle-length red skirt with matching jacket the instant the door opened. He didn't need to see her any closer to know that her eyes were green and her lips were naturally rosy rather than painted.

He immediately stood and called out, "Miss Kitty Belle!"

She started at the sound of her name, but recognizing the voice, replied, "Why, I do declare, Mr. Cheyenne Walker!" and headed toward his voice, her eyes not yet adjusted to the relative darkness inside the cantina after the brilliance of the outside sun. She swayed into the chair he gallantly held out for her—also placed where she could see the door and windows. Their knees almost touched under the table.

"The cool air within is a great relief," she said. "As I expected would be the case when I espied the mirrored tower above." The instant she was settled, he shook out a clean bandanna for her to blot the perspiration from her brow.

"I recommend the small beer to rinse the dust of the trail from your throat," he said, and added, "the burritos here are the best I've had." He pushed his plate aside; he'd continue with his dinner when Miss Kitty was served.

"But Burritos are Tex-Mex rather than Mexican," she objected, "and this is a Mexican cantina."

"Very true. But so many Texicans are moving into El Paso that Falina has added Tex-Mex to her menu to satisfy them."

"In that case," she said looking at the young woman who approached the table, "I would like chicken fajitas, along with the recommended small beer."

"Si, senora." the young woman said and scurried to the kitchen to place the order and fetch a small beer.

"Am I correct in assuming that you are staying at the Del Norte hotel?" Walker asked while they awaited Miss Kitty's small beer.

"I am so domiciled for my stay here as it appears to be the only electrified lodging in town." Then, "Gracias," to the senorita who just then placed a cold glass on the table by her left hand. Back to Walker, "How come you happen to be in El Paso?" she asked over the rim of her glass.

He shook his head. "After those murderous spirits that photographer conjured in Zapotec, I found myself at unease in New Mexico Territory and decided to travel east for a time." He shrugged.

"I hadn't been in Texas for some while, so... And what brings you here?"

"Mr. Pinkerton received word of strange deaths and livestock mutilations in this corner of Texas. Being aware of the mystical nature of some of the cases I've worked on, he dispatched me to investigate."

"And you didn't send a Babbage summoning me?" Walker asked, with raised eyebrows.

She graced him with a slight smile. "Had I discovered mystical forces at work here, I most assuredly would have attempted to entice you to join me. As it is..." she broke off as her fajita dishes were placed on the table. "After our sojourn," she pointed at his burrito plate, "we can discuss how you might be of assistance in the investigation."

Later, sated from their meal, they quietly discussed what to do. First, they headed to the office of the county sheriff. When they found his office untenanted, they went a short distance down the street to visit the *Corner Gazette*, El Paso's newspaper.

Unlike the loud *klickety-klatter* made by the hand-cranked printing press at the *Zapotec Herald*, a soft *swish-swish* came through the open door of the *Corner Gazette's* office. Miss Kitty Belle rapped on the doorjamb before stepping inside, leading Cheyenne Walker into the room. It was noticeably less hot inside than it had been outside. A glance upward disclosed an array of small, slowly rotating ceiling fans that drew hot air up and let the cooler air near the ceiling drop down.

An aproned man stood hunched over a table, scraping a sheet of foolscap. He glanced up at their entrance and peeled the paper off its bed of set type. "Be right with you folks," he said as he pinned the foolscap to one of several lines strung across the room. Satisfied that it was unwrinkled and not fluttering in the slight downdraft, he turned to his visitors and wiped his hands on his apron. He didn't offer his ink-stained hand to shake.

"I'm Billy Locke," he addressed them. "You," he looked at Walker, "I know. You're the gambling man who isn't much playing at cards. But I haven't made your acquaintance," he said to Kitty Belle.

"I'm Pinkerton Agent Miss Kitty Belle," she said, producing her identification.

"Ah, yes, I'd heard that the Pinkertons were sending an agent to suss out the cause behind our recent killings and sheep slaughters." He cocked his head in momentary thought, then, "I've also seen reports that a Pinkerton and a gambling man oft times work together on strange crimes." He gave them a sheepish grin. "Come to think of it, I've even re-printed such a story or two. Yes, I'm mighty pleased to make your acquaintance."

"It appears our reputation precedes us," Walker said. "It's not a rumor. We are they."

"And you are correct about my purpose in visiting El Paso. What can you tell us about the killings?" Kitty Belle asked.

"Not a lot to tell. Over the past three months a dozen cowboys out looking for strays have come to a gruesome end on the range. Their corpses were partially eaten, as by puma or wolves. But they looked like the buzzards hadn't gotten to them yet. And by current count, two or three dozen sheep were also found with their throats and bellies torn out. The buzzards had shorn their meat almost to the bone, and coyotes crunched the bones to get at the morrow."

"And it's always sheep, not cattle they were looking for?" Kitty Belle asked.

Locke nodded. "Yes. We have many sheep ranches in this area. The only cattle ranch mostly raises beefs for the abattoir and butcher shop."

"If the killed men were all shepherds," Walker asked, "why are they called cowboys?"

Locke shrugged. "Hear tell, we're all cowboys out here anymore. Anyway, that's what the Buffalo Soldiers called the first one they found. The name stuck."

"Buffalo Soldiers… A colored company from the 9th Cavalry is stationed at Fort Bliss," Walker remarked. "They conduct patrols in this corner of Texas, and even some into New Mexico. I've seen them riding through town."

"Are all the killings in one area?" Kitty Belle asked, ignoring the explanation.

"No ma'am. Some are to the north of town, some northeast, and a couple have been to the west."

"Did they start in the northeast and are working their way westward?"

Locke shook his head. "They've been scattered about in random directions and distances, near as we can tell. The closest was little more 'n a mile north of town, and the farthest about ten miles northwest." He shook his head again. "I've been plotting them on a Geological Corps Survey map, but I can't make hide nor sense of it." He opened a wide, shallow drawer under his worktable and slid out a large sheet of paper. "See?" he said, gesturing at the map. He stepped aside so Walker and Belle could have unimpeded access.

There were many locations marked, each with a date. Twelve had the name of the unfortunate cowboy whose corpse was discovered at that location, as close apart in time as three days and as distant as two weeks. The dates seemed to be as randomly spaced as were the locations. The other locations indicated where only sheep had been found.

Kitty Belle withdrew a lead pencil and notebook from her purse and began jotting down dates and approximate locations. Finished, she studied her notes and nodded. "Yes, there seems neither rhyme nor reason of a pattern to the killings." She handed the notebook to Walker.

He looked it over and shook his head, saying, "Most peculiar."

Miss Kitty mused for a moment, then asked, "Did anything out of the ordinary take place before the killings began?"

Locke shook his head again. "Only the normal rough and tumble of a frontier town."

"What about Indians," Walker asked. "Aren't there Apache in this region?"

"Yes." Locke started, surprised by the question. "I hadn't considered them in regard to Miss Belle's question. There was a band of Mescalero Apache encamped near the New Mexico border. They decamped when the Federal government established a reservation for them in New Mexico."

"And it was soon after that when the killings began?"

Locke looked from one to the other, not sure whether he should direct his response to Walker, who had presented the question, or to Kitty Belle, whom he believed was properly in charge of the inquiry. Ultimately, he replied to the space between them:

"Not immediately. It was, I believe..." he broke off to leaf through the sheets of paper in a cabinet. "Ah, yes, here we are." He opened up a folded copy of the *Corner Gazette*. "The Apache left for their new reservation fourteen weeks ago. The first killing, a sheep, was discovered two weeks later. The first deceased cowboy three days after." He got a distant look in his eye. "I never considered a connection. Do you think there might be such?"

Miss Kitty didn't shrug, but it hung there in her voice when she answered "I do not know. But whether there is, or something else is the cause, I intend to find out." She glanced to her side. "With the assistance of Mr. Cheyenne Walker, of course."

Sheriff Ken Goode didn't look pleased to see his visitors when Cheyenne Walker arrived at the town office with Miss Kitty Belle. "If'n ya'd got here yestadee," he said gruffly, "ya might could a gone on the grass with me to 'vestigate another cowboy with his throat ripped right out, like what them Buff'lo Sojers found startin' 'bout three months ago." The twist in the sheriff's lips suggested he didn't approve of the black soldiers. He shook his head. "Couldn't'a bin there more'n a day or so. This makes thirteen cowboys bin found now."

"What about the cowboy's horse," Kitty Belle asked.

'It must'a run off a'for the cowboy got hisself kilt."

Walker nodded. "Did it run off? In all the instances where the Buffalo soldiers found dead cowboys, their horses had run until they collapsed from exhaustion, and subsequently were devoured by whatever chased them."

"I knows thet. An' there warn't no trace of what kilt 'em." He shook his head. "As that's what happened ever time the Buff'lo Sojers went looking, I didn't see no profit in me chasing down another dead horse." He shrugged again. 'Jis one more p'culiar thing 'bout these here killin's."

"Mr. Locke at the *Corner Gazette* said a band of Mescalero moved to a new reservation in New Mexico a fortnight before the mysterious sheep killings and murders began," Miss Kitty said, seeking confirmation.

"Ak'chul, it was a p'toon a them Buff'lo Sojers herded them Mescaleros to their reservation." The word Goode used to describe the escort provided to the Indians suggested he had no higher regard for them than he had for the black cavalrymen. He snorted. "'Fortnight.' Thas a right fancy word t' be slingin' round here. But yeah, thas 'bout when it started. Did Mr. Locke make mention of the Dine what was with them 'Paches?"

"Nossir," Walker said, tipping his head to the side in thought.

Kitty Belle cast a quick glance his way, wondering what had just occurred to him, but the sheriff continued before either of them could speak.

"One a them Dine, he was a bad 'un. A young feller, always gettin' drunk an' goin' 'round layin' curses on folk—whites, as well as Mexicans and Injuns. You'd a thunk he was some kind'a pagan priest, or sumpin else ungodlike." He shook his head. "Ya never know what's goin' on in the heads a them heathens. If'n he weren't always so fallin' down drunk, I like would'a had t' arrest him and charge him with makin' teroristic threats, or some such. But," he shrugged, "what ya gonna do with some Injun kain't hold his likker, 'cept lock 'im inna hoosegow t' sleep it off. Either that or string 'im up." He shook his head. "Mos' folks round here doan take kindly to lynching fer gettin' drunk. Horse thievin,' though, thas diff'rent."

"What was his name, that drunk Navaho? Do you know?" Walker asked.

Goode snorted. "Less he's Chief Red Cloud or some 'un like that, who cares?"

"Surely the ranchers are angered about losing so many men and sheep," Kitty Belle said. "Are they agitating for you to take action?"

"'Deed they are. Some of 'em are threat'ning to go t' the gov-'ner." He *harumphed*. "Not much joy fer 'em there. The gov'ner's a cattleman, don't hold much with sheeps." He just shook his head, as though suddenly waking from a nap. "Come t' think of it, they's havin' a meetin' t'night at the Holed Ace saloon, on acounter it's the onlyst place big enough t' hold alla them. You should oughta come. Seven o'clock. If'n they know the Pinkertons are on it, might could take some pressure off'n me."

Sheriff Ken Goode had said he found the latest deceased cowboy "on the grass," but there was little that could be properly called "grass" in the scrub desert through which a squad of Buffalo Soldiers from Company L of the 9th Cavalry patrolled. Most of what grew there was agave and desert spoon, with splashes of color provided by scattered false yucca plants. An infrequent cottonwood tree rose above the scrub, usually near a dry arroyo.

Private James Washington, riding scout ahead of his squad, reined in and sat for a moment looking at the gruesome sight that had stopped him, then twirled his arm over his head, signaling the rest of the squad to join him.

"Got another one, Sarge," he said when Sergeant Grant joined him.

Sergeant Grant looked at the bloodied, mangled corpse laying a few yards away and shook his head. "Corporal Pike, pair off the rest of the squad to search this area for more bodies or other sign."

"Right, Sarge." Pike began shouting orders to the rest of the squad, pairing them off two by two and sending them in different directions to search the ground a quarter mile out from the body of the dead cowboy.

"And look for sign!" Grant shouted after them. Then, almost to himself, "Maybe this time we can find more than a horse's trail to follow." He spat to the side. "Why me?" he wondered. This was the third time his squad had found one of these bodies, one more than the rest of the company combined. He'd have to wrap the corpse in a Macintosh and take it back to the undertaker in El Paso. It didn't matter that this cowboy had been a white man, Washington and his men would treat the remains with the same respect that they had the black cowboy they'd come across two weeks earlier. He looked to the west, toward the Franklin Mountains, and hoped his squad would patrol there next. So far, no bodies had been found in the mountains.

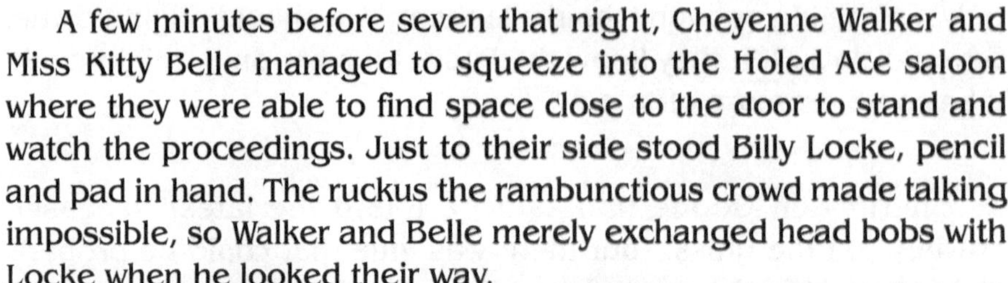

A few minutes before seven that night, Cheyenne Walker and Miss Kitty Belle managed to squeeze into the Holed Ace saloon where they were able to find space close to the door to stand and watch the proceedings. Just to their side stood Billy Locke, pencil and pad in hand. The ruckus the rambunctious crowd made talking impossible, so Walker and Belle merely exchanged head bobs with Locke when he looked their way.

"This here meeting of the El Paso Shepherds Association will now come to order!" Judge Jim Bean roared as he hammered his gavel on the block of wood set on the saloon's bar for that purpose, behind which he sat on a high stool. "If you don't have your drinks now, you're going to be dry on account of the bar's closed until the meeting's over.

"Order, I said!" roaring over the shouted objections. "You knew that coming in, and you knew the meeting was set for seven PM sharp. I'll have you know I held off gaveling the meeting to order until ten minutes after to give you more time to get your whiskey or beer. If you couldn't get your drinks before then, that's your fault. If there are any further interruptions, I'll instruct Sheriff Goode to lock you in his jail until tomorrow, and then you will have to wait until then to get a drink. So shut up!" He again slammed his gavel onto the wood block, this time with enough force to send it skittering several feet down the bar. He ignored the muttered complaints about the "worthless" sheriff who had so far failed to put a stop to the slaughters of their sheep. He also ignored the glum expression on the face of Jonas Sasper, the owner of the Holed Ace, despondent because of the business he was losing while the bar was closed.

"Yes Mr. Kincade, you have something to say?" The judge recognized the president of the association, a burly man whose white hair and fluffy beard resembled the wool of a sheep that was due for a shearing.

"I sure do, yer honor." Kincade's voice rumbled out of his chest in a timber unsuggested by the sheep-like appearance of his locks and whiskers. "Jist a few months ago I had more'n 5,000 sheep. As of yesterday, I was down more than a hundred head. Pret' near everybody in this room knows the value of a hundred sheep. For some, it means the difference between makin' it for another year and goin' bust."

He paused to let murmurs of agreement run their course among the sheepherders, as some of them did have herds so small that a loss of a hundred head of sheep could cost them their ranches.

"The sheriff doesn't have enough deputies to keep watch on the entire county," he continued. "The Buffalo Soldiers help some, but one troop ain't enough neither. And that company from the 15th Infantry can't do nothin' to stop the depredations on account of they're foot sojers, not horse sojers.

"What I think this comes down to is, we gotta go to the governor and tell him to send in the Texas Rangers."

That brought shouts of agreement from the other sheep men. But Judge Bean shook his head. "Now you know the same as me that the governor is a cattle. Any help he gives us here will be too little, and won't last long enough to solve the problem. I think Sheriff Goode should deputize all of you and your hands. All of you, combined with the Buffalo Soldiers just might be enough to take care of the problem once and for all. What say you?" He directed that last at the sheriff over the loudly shouted objections from the sheep ranchers.

Goode loudly cleared his throat before answering. "Yer Honor, I think that's a mighty fine ideer. But even if the sheep men would be willin', which I sort'er doubt they would, that's a might wily coyote we got out there. Even if'n they caught him, I kinder spec they'd git kilt themownselfs. Now, I think we should let them decide for their ownselves if they are willing to have them and their hands deputized."

Judge Bean noticed a hand in the back of the assembly waving at him. "Yes, Mr. Locke. Do you have something to contribute to this meeting?"

"Yessir, Your Honor, I do. Judge Bean, you might have noticed we have a couple strangers here."

The judge nodded and gestured for the newspaperman to continue.

"Well, sir, the lady is Miss Kitty Belle of the Pinkerton Agency." He paused while a susurration of murmurs ran through the crowd.

Judge Bean glared at the noisemakers and raised his gavel as if to hammer it down on the wooden block, which Sasper had moved back to protect his bar top. Everyone instantly grew quiet, and the judge lowered his gavel, although kept his hand on it—just in case.

"Now Mr. Locke, it's all well and good to have a Pinkerton here in town. But surely you aren't suggesting that she can do all by herself what we know an entire company of Buffalo Soldiers can't do."

"Nossir, nossir, that's not at all what I'm suggesting." He shook his head sharply, looking sheepishly at Walker and Belle before continuing. "Well, your Honor, I guess I am suggesting exactly that. You have to admit, this whole situation, the killings and all, do seem to not be entirely natural. You see, sir, the well-dressed gentleman standing next to Miss Belle is Mr. Cheyenne Walker—"

"Cheyenne Walker?" Judge Bean interrupted. "That name sounds familiar." He looked at Walker. "I think I've seen it somewhere. Maybe on a wanted poster. Hmm?"

Walker cooly answered, "I don't think so, your Honor. I'm sure there are some gamblers who'd like to find me because I out-played them at cards, but to the best of my knowledge no lawman has called a search for me."

"Umm hmm. We'll see. Anyway, Mr. Locke, you were saying?"

"Yessir. Miss Kitty Belle and Mr. Cheyenne Walker, working together, have encountered several instances of what might be called supernatural events. In each case, they have brought them to successful conclusions. You might recognize the names of Miss Belle and Mr. Walker from reading *The Corner Gazette*. I have printed a story or two about their exploits."

The judge *harumphed* again, not completely convinced that Walker's name didn't grace a wanted poster somewhere, but he was willing to put his suspicion aside for the time being.

"You may continue, Mr. Locke."

"Well, your Honor, sir, given what they've done in the past, I think that maybe, just maybe, they could get to the bottom of these mysterious killings!"

Judge Bean cast a doubtful eye first at the two outsiders, then at Locke. "You think that, do you?"

"Yessir, I do."

"And what think you?" to Walker and Belle.

"Your Honor," Belle's voice rang clear in the room, "Mr. Pinkerton did dispatch me to investigate these killings, word of which had reached him in Chicago. If," she looked to her side: "Mr. Walker is willing to assist me in my investigation I'm willing to learn what I can find."

Walker cleared his throat before replying without looking at Miss Kitty. "If it is satisfactory to you, your Honor, I am more than willing to join with Miss Belle in this endeavor."

Judge Bean raised his gavel preparatory to adjourning the meeting when Belle stopped him with a question to the assemblage.

"Have any others gone missing whilst out searching for missing sheep?"

"That happens alla time, missy," Kincade said. "So many of the men we hire are saddle tramps, men just passing through what stops fer long enough to make a few bucks, then keep goin' on." He dismissively shrugged. Other sheep men shouted their agreement.

"So, there could be more bodies out there that simply haven't been found yet?"

"I guess," Kincade reluctantly admitted. "Three er four of a 'em mebbe."

"One more thing," Walker interjected. "All the bodies that have been found have been lone men, none in pairs or groups. So, until this problem is resolved, I strongly suggest that no one goes out alone to track down missing sheep."

Judge Bean again cracked gavel hard enough to send the block skittering down the bar to cut off the chorus of complaints at Walker's suggestion.

"What the man says is only common sense," the judge roared. "Send your searchers out two by two, not one at a time. We don't need more rent-apart bodies moldering out on the grass.

"As county judge, I hereby appoint Pinkerton Agent Belle and Mr. Cheyenne Walker to investigate these killings, and hopefully draw them to a satisfactory solution. Satisfactory to all save the poor souls that have been killed.

"This meeting is hereby adjourned. "Mr. Sasper, kindly open the bar, and serve me a glass of your finest top-shelf whiskey.

⟶◦❂◦⟵

At Fort Bliss, Cheyenne Walker and Miss Kitty Belle were ushered into the commanding officer's office.

Colonel John Harris carefully examined Kitty Belle's identification before asking, "And what brings the Pinkerton Agency to this remote corner of Texas?" He didn't invite them to sit, although there was a bench opposite his desk. "And the gambling man standing next to you?"

"Colonel, I have on occasion assisted Miss Kitty Belle on her investigations in the Southwest territories," Walker answered.

Harris nodded without comment on Walker's explanation, but asked another question of Kitty Belle. "In what manner do you think the United States Army should be involved in your investigation?"

"The sheriff has informed me that your Buffalo Soldiers have found several of the poor souls." In response to Colonel Harris' rudeness in not making an offer for them to sit, she deliberately omitted the honorific "sir" when she answered. "I would be very appreciative if one of the Buffalo Soldiers could show me—*us*—where some of the bodies have been found."

"Do I understand you correctly, that you are asking for the United States Army to assist you in your investigation?"

"I am not asking for assistance in my investigation, I merely want to be shown a place from which we can begin our detecting."

Hruumph. "You are mounted?"

"Yes, we are."

"If you don't object to spending most of a day wandering in this god-forsaken wilderness, be here half an hour after dawn tomorrow and you can accompany a squad of Buffalo Soldiers when it goes on patrol."

"Colonel, I have lived most of my life in the 'god-forsaken wilderness' that is the Southwest," Walker said. "And Miss Belle has been over much of it as well. We will be here."

Caleb Stuggs wasn't anybody in particular. Just another saddle tramp cowboy wandering from ranch to ranch, working for a week or a month here, a week or a month there. Wherever he could find employment with a cattle boss who needed an extra hand for a time. His current job wasn't on a cattle ranch, but on a sheep ranch. He wasn't happy with this—he didn't like the way the sheep ate the grass all the way to the roots, leaving the ground bare.

But here he was, out on the prairie, looking for a sheep that had wandered off. He had half a mind to just keep going, leave the lost sheep to the coyotes. As he looked about for the missing sheep, he saw on a low mesa in the middle distance what he took to be an Indian looking back at him. That was a surprise, as he'd heard the local Apaches had been moved to a reservation in New Mexico. He wasn't concerned, though. There hadn't been any trouble that he'd heard of between the Indians and the whites. Except for that Navaho who kept getting drunk and cursing people. And that never led to anything more than shouts. So, unless there were some Comanche he hadn't heard about in the area, a lone Indian, if that was in fact what he saw, was nothing to worry about.

Still, he was about done with sheep. The horse he rode belonged to the ranch, but the saddle and bedroll were his. He was owed a couple weeks pay, so if he just kept going it wasn't like he was stealing the horse. *Not really,* he thought.

It was getting on dark, so he decided to make himself a fire, eat some of the beans and salt pork he had in his saddlebag, and sleep on whether to continue looking for the sheep in the morning, or to move on. He was halfway through his cold dinner when his hobbled horse started whinnying and stomping its hooves.

He went to the mare to stroke her neck and settle her. "What's the matter, girl? Do you smell coyotes? I don't think they'll come close to the fire, so you just stay by me and there won't be any trouble."

The mare suddenly screamed. She bucked, kicked back, and flailed hard enough with her front legs to kick off the hobbles, knocking him to the ground in the process.

"What?" Stuggs yelped as she bolted. Before he could regain his feet, a blood-curdling shriek spun him in the direction opposite the way the horse had run.

Before he could react to the sight that met his vision, he was repelled by the stench radiating from it. He scrambled back until he was able to gain his feet. The creature that had so frightened his horse and himself was shaped half like a man, half like a bear. It was covered with long lank hair and stood a full head shorter than Stuggs. He looked around manically for his gun—he had no doubt that the beast could rend him in a grapple. Spying his weapon wrapped in his spare shirt, next to his opened bedroll, he dove for it. The shrieking beast pounced, landing on Stuggs' back, driving the wind from his lungs. Stuggs reached for his gun as the shaggy man-bear tore at his back. Hewas barely conscious of what was happening when the monster flipped him onto his back and tore out his throat. He never felt it eviscerate him.

After it finished, the creature leaped into the air and vanished. In its place a giant owl flew after the galloping mare. The owl jabbed a talon into the haunch of the galloping horse, not to cripple it but to keep it running in panic. When the horse finally collapsed with its heart beating to burst, the owl landed on it, sinking its talons into its belly, and ripping at its throat with its beak. The owl pointed its head at the moon and let out an unearthly cry, summoning coyotes to the feast before flapping away into the night.

"Miz Belle, Mr. Walker," Sergeant Malakai Grant greeted them when they entered the parade ground of the fort soon after dawn the next day. "I'm Sergeant Grant. I understand you are to accompany my patrol and that you want to see where we found the bodies of the murdered cowboys."

He looked over these two civilians whose care had been given over to him. In his experience, most civilians weren't up to the rigors of the prairie, unless they were riding in a carriage, and often not even then. These two, though, might be exceptions. The man sat his horse like he belonged on one; his blue canvas duster had seen use, and his slouch hat spoke of time spent in the sun. The woman, in a divided skirt, rode her horse astraddle like a man, rather than on a side-saddle. Her white linen duster, though new, was a practical garment. She also wore a slouch hat. Both were armed. Walker had a very long-barreled .45 in a holster on his right hip. The Pinkerton agent carried a Colt Peacemaker in a holster draped over her saddle horn. While neither paid any particular attention to their firearms, both gave the impression that they knew how to use them.

"I'm pleased to meet you, sergeant," Kitty Belle said. "Mr. Locke at the *Corner Gazette* has spoken well of you."

Grant hesitated before taking her hand when she extended it to shake as a man would—women seldom shook hands, and then only with other women. But a white woman offering to shake hands with a colored man!

The crunch of marching boots across the parade ground announced the arrival of Colonel Harris.

"You arrived on time," Harris said, surprise evident in his voice.

"We said we would," Kitty Belle responded.

"So, you did. Sergeant, you are to conduct these two civilians to the most recent location where remains were found. That is the extent of your obligation to them, and they are not to detour you on your patrol. Is that understood?"

"Yessir."

"That's all we asked for," Walker said.

"Very well. Sergeant, do they meet muster?"

"Yessir, I do believe they are ready to ride."

"Then God be with you." Without bothering to return Grant's salute, Harris turned about and marched back toward the cooled air in his office.

Walker watched him go with a raised eyebrow but said nothing.

Kitty Belle ignored the departing colonel altogether. "We have had breakfast, sergeant. If you and your men have eaten, I see no reason to delay our departure."

"Yes, ma'am. We are ready to go." He barked a command, and the men of his squad mounted up and fell in on him. "Miz Belle, Mr. Walker," Grant said, "If you are ready?"

Walker had mounted with the cavalrymen; Belle was just swinging onto her saddle.

Grant nodded, then said, "Jefferson, you know where we are going. Lead out!"

"Right, Sarge," Private Zebulon Jefferson answered, and gave heel to his mount. The squad filed in good order two by two through the open gate of Fort Bliss and headed northeast.

Private Jefferson, riding a hundred yards ahead of the rest of the short column suddenly veered from the route he'd been on and cantered a short distance to his right front. he looked at the ground for a moment, then turned about and galloped.

"Sarge, we got another one," he reported.

"Corporal Pike, take charge. Keep everyone here." He added to Kitty Belle and Cheyenne Walker, "Come with us." Then to Jefferson, "Show me."

A moment later, he stood on his saddle looking at the remains of another eviscerated cowboy.

"They have all been like this?" Miss Kitty asked when she'd taken in the horrible sight.

"Yes, ma'am," Grant said softly. Then firmly ordered, "Jefferson, go back to Corporal Pike. Tell him to pair the men off and start searching the ground, beginning a hundred yards from here. Search for any tracks or other sign. Same as before."

"Right, Sarge." Jefferson turned his horse about and headed back. He didn't hear Grant's muttered, "Maybe this time we'll find something."

But all they found was the tracks made by Caleb Stuggs' horse on its way into the campsite, the brief fight when the cowboy was killed, and where the horse bolted away.

"Corporal Pike, take one man and see where that horse went."

Pike shook his head. "I 'spect we'll find what we did afore. A dead horse coyotes and buzzards been feeding on."

Grant gave Pike a hard look.

"Right, Sarge. Sam, come with me." The two Buffalo Soldiers trotted off, following the track of the panicked horse. They were back in something more than an hour.

Except—Cheyenne Walker looked at the ground for a short distance opposite the direction from which the frightened mare fled and slowly meandered that way.

"We found the horse, a mare," Corporal Pike reported. "Hadn't been there too long. Coyotes and buzzards was still fightin' over her."

"Did anybody notice this?" Walker asked, calling out from a good distance.

"What do you have?" Sergeant Grant asked as he joined Walker. He looked at what the gambling man pointed out. "Looks like talon marks. But it takes a mighty big bird to make scratches that big."

Walker took a deep breath, because what he was about to say was going to sound outrageous.

"I think what we might be dealing with here is a Skinwalker."

Grant snorted. "Skinwalker! That's just Navaho superstition."

"How does that explain what we have here?" Miss Kitty asked. "And what do the talon scratches have to do with it?"

"According to the Navajo, Skinwalkers are also shape-changers. I suspect the Skinwalker flew in as a bird, killed the cowboy, then turned back into a bird and chased his horse until the horse's heart burst." He shrugged. "That explains everything we know about these killings"

"But these killings are pure evil," Grant said. "What little I've heard, Skinwalkers only kill people who see them. I don't think all these dead cowboys could have seen them by accident."

Walker nodded. "I've heard the same. According to all I've heard about Skinwalkers, they don't become pure evil until they kill a close relative."

"Then we need to find out if that Navaho shaman is still with the Mescalero, and if his mother is still there even if he isn't," Kitty Belle said.

Grant snorted again. "Going to the Navajo reservation would be a waste of time. Even if that shaman isn't still there, Skinwalkers are just superstition, they're not real."

"Sergeant Grant, I assure you, Miss Belle and I have seen things that beggar belief, things that some would call impossible—or superstition."

"Indeed, sergeant," Miss Kitty added, "not only superstition, but supernatural as well."

"The Lord God and His Saints?"

Kitty Belle shook her head. "Not that God nor those saints."

"Coyote and Raven," Cheyenne Walker added.

Grant looked from one to the other, hardly able to believe his ears, that these two white people were talking about Indian superstitions as if they were the Lord's own truth. He shook his head in disbelief, not only at what they had said, but at what he was about to say.

"There is a sutler who comes to Fort Bliss every two weeks. He also visits the Apache reservation in New Mexico. He should be here in the next couple of days. We can ask him then."

Late the next afternoon, Private Zebulon Jefferson found Cheyenne Walker and Miss Kitty Belle having dinner at Falina's Cantina.

"Miz Belle, Mr. Walker. Ma'am, sir, Sar'nt Grant sent me to tell you Mr. Tal Merca is at the fort, if you want to talk to him."

"Who might Mr. Tal Merca be?" Kitty Belle asked.

"Oh, yes. You don't know. "Mr. Tal Mercer is the sutler. And he was at the reservation, I heard him say that."

"Thank you, Private Jefferson," Miss Kitty said. She looked at the dinner that she and Walker had almost finished. "Have you had dinner yet?"

Jefferson's eyes lit up at the question. "No, ma'am. Evening chow hadn't been called yet when Mr. Merca came to fort and Sar'nt Grant sent me to tell you."

"Well, we can't have you missing your dinner," Walker said. Order whatever you want here and I'll pay for it." He signaled the young senorita to take care of the Buffalo Soldier. "Miss Kitty and I will go to the fort now." He looked at Kitty Belle for confirmation.

"The minute we finish our dinner," she said, and set to.

Minutes later, their dinners finished, and Jefferson's ordered and paid for, they took their leave.

When Cheyenne Walker and Miss Kitty Belle dismounted at a hitching post on the edge of the Fort Bliss parade ground, they saw Sergeant Grant heading toward them. In his wake waddled a huge man; curtains of fat seemed to drape off him like blubber on a whale.

"Miz Belle, Mr. Walker," Grant said when he reached them. He half-turned to his rear and held out a hand to indicate the rapidly approaching stranger. "This is Mr. Tal Merca, the sutler."

"Miz Belle, Mr. Walker," Merca rasped, sounding winded. He assayed a clumsy bow to Miss Kitty and stuck a plump hand out to Walker.

"That's a powerful grip you've got there, Mr. Merca," Walker said while shaking the sutler's hand. He resisted the urge to flex his hand to work out the pain from the crushing grip Merca had given him.

"I have t' be strong," Merca replied. "Half the time when I load or unload my wagon, I got to do it all by my alone self. Takes some strength to heave them drums of beans and salt pork."

Walker looked at the mess hall, where several fifty-five-gallon barrels had been lined up for the cook-crew to move inside. "I believe you," Walker said.

"Sar'nt Grant tells me you wants to know 'bout that Navajo medicine man what went to the rez with them Mescalero." While he talked his eyes kept flitting to the barrels sitting unattended outside the mess hall.

"Indeed, Mr. Merca, I would very much like to know if that Dine is still with the Apache."

Merca shook his head, sending his jowls flapping side to side. "Way I heard it, that medicine man acted up at the 'Paches the same as he did to the white folks and Mexicans in El Paso. The Mescalero wasn't putting up with that, no sir. So, they kicked him out, him and his mother, too." He jittered while delivering this speech and kept glancing at the barrels.

"You seem nervous, Mr. Merca," Kitty Belle said. "Is there a problem?"

"Ma'am, them barrels are sitting out in the sun. The mess sar'nt ain't signed for 'em yet. If they goes bad sitting in the sun, I don't get paid for 'em."

"We wouldn't want that to happen, sir, so we won't detain you much longer. But we do have another question or two."

"Yes'm." Merca's eyes bulged in his anxiety to have the mess sergeant sign for the barrels.

"So, the medicine man and his mother haven't been seen since?"

"No, ma'am." He hesitated, looking toward the northwest. "Funny thing, there. Couple a months back, on my way from the rez to here I come across a body on the grass tween the rez and here. Scavengers got to it so clean I couldn't tell who it might'a been, 'cept the scraps of clothing scatted around tole me it was prob'ly a woman." He shrugged. "Might could'a been the medicine man's mother."

"Do you know the medicine man's name?" Walker asked.

"Some Navaho name Itsey, or Yahoo or something like that."

Walker thought for a moment, thinking of what he remembered of Navaho names. "Might it have been Yeitso?" he asked.

"Might well have been that, yessir."

"Thank you, Mr. Merca. You've been very helpful. Now get that mess sergeant to sign for your victuals."

"Glad to help," Mercer said as he waddled as briskly as he could toward the mess hall.

"What are you thinking, Mr. Walker?" Kitty Belle asked.

Walker looked to the northwest. "I think Yeitso is a Skinwalker. I think the body Mr. Merca found was his mother." He looked at Miss Kitty Belle. "Skinwalkers are not bad, just very dangerous. But according to what I've heard, once they've killed a close relative, they become evil. Whatever killed those cowboys is undoubtedly evil.

Three days later, Sergeant Malakai Grant and his Buffalo Soldiers escorted Cheyenne Walker and Kitty Belle to where the horse of the unfortunate Caleb Stuggs had been found.

"Been picked pretty clean," Grant observed when they reached the remains. The horse's bones were scattered about, and many were broken to give the scavengers access to their marrow.

"Nothing goes to waste out here," Walker agreed.

"I thank you greatly for bringing us this far," Miss Kitty said. "Now you can continue your patrol so your Colonel doesn't get upset with you."

"You're sure the two of you will be all right on your own?" Grant asked somewhat dubiously.

"We've been on our own in some strange and dangerous places in past times," Walker said. "This should be no different."

"But if you're right about the Skinwalker..."

"It's only attacked lone cowboys. There are two of us, "Miss Kitty said. "We are unlikely to be in any particular danger."

Halfway through the next afternoon, only a few hundred yards from a low mesa, Cheyenne Walker, looking past Miss Kitty Belle, abruptly said, "Don't turn, don't look behind yourself."

She didn't flinch or look, just asked, "Why not? What do you see?"

"I see something—or someone—on top of that mesa. Off to the left. If it's the Skinwalker, he knows I've seen him. You haven't. I think if we act like we're having a fight and you leave in a huff, he'll come after me and leave you alone."

"But he'll kill you!" she objected.

Walker shook his head. "I know his name. That's the first and most important thing in defeating a Skinwalker." He hunched up his shoulders as though he was shouting at her. "So go!"

"If that's the way you feel about it," she said, leaning toward him with her hands bent in like claws to strike at him.

"Yes, it is!" he yelled with his chest puffed out looking like he was roaring at her.

"So how are you going to keep from getting killed? So, what if you know his name? How are you going to keep him from swooping down on you like he did to that cowboy?"

Walker violently shook his head. "I'll sit with my back to that cottonwood where we sat out of the sun to have our luncheon. He won't be able to swoop in on me, he'll have to come to ground then the advantage will be mine. The trunk of that tree is wide enough he won't be able to come at me from behind, he'll have to be where I can see him." He drew his pistol and waved it in what he hoped looked like a threat. "He's not immune to .45 caliber bullets."

Kitty Belle leaned back from him. "All right, I'll go. But I'm not going to be far."

"Stay out of sight."

"I will." She twisted from him, careful to not look in the direction of the mesa, and stomped off to her horse, which she mounted and cantered off without looking back.

Walker stared after her, then looked down. "You left your bed roll," he muttered. Then he picked up his own and went to the cottonwood and settled for what he expected to be a long wait for sundown, still a few hours off. While he waited, he wracked his brain for everything he could remember about Skinwalkers.

Before the stars started winking into existence, he stirred the ashes over which he and Miss Kitty Belle had heated their luncheon until there was a pile of fine white ash. He drew his Buntline Special and unloaded it, one round at a time, and carefully coated the bullets in a fine coating of the white ash before inserting them back into the cylinder. *I'm going to have to give my pistol a good cleaning after this,*" he thought.

Now ready, with his bullets coated with white ash as the legends said, he resumed his patient wait.

When the night had turned full dark with a quarter moon rising, he thought he heard a faint *whooshing*, like the wings of a huge bird breaking its landward plummet. There was a crashing in the branches overhead, and snapped twigs fell to the ground. An angry *Whoo-o-o* sounded from the canopy, followed by a moving rustling in the branches, going from almost directly from above to the edge of the canopy to Walker's front. He pointed the muzzle of his long-barreled .45 in that direction and rolled from sitting with his back to the cottonwood's wide trunk to his knees.

A *thunk!* just to the side of straight ahead turned Walker's eyes to a strange sight. A man-like shape about four feet tall and covered in long hair recovered from its drop, turning in a sprinter's crouch.

But before it could start its run, Walker shouted, "Yeitso, I know you!"

The Skinwalker froze in place. Moonlight glittered off its hate-filled eyes as it stared at the man who spoke his name. Then it threw its head back and screeched its frustration and anger.

Walker sat back on one foot and raised the other knee. He put his elbows on that knee to steady his aim, which he put straight on the Skinwalker's open mouth. At almost the same instant, he heard the *Bang!* of another pistol to his left front. The Skinwalker's head jerked back and to the right before Walker could turn to see where the other shot came from.

He saw Kitty Belle rising to her feet. a thin line of smoke dribbled up from the muzzle of her Peacemaker. Her duster no longer looked clean, much less new.

"Did we kill it?" she shouted.

"I suspect so. We both made head shots. Those are supposed to work."

"Good." She started toward the body.

"Careful," Walker cautioned as he also headed toward the Skinwalker. "It might still be alive." He reached the body first, but didn't say anything until Kitty Belle joined him. Up close they could see that the long hair covering the body was greasy. They stood silent for a moment, watching the corpse of the Skinwalker that had once been the Navajo shaman Yeitso slowly disintegrate.

"I think that solves the problem of murdered cowboys and slaughtered sheep," The Pinkerton agent said. "They will be pleased to get my report in Chicago."

"Where had you gone?" Walker asked when they were mounted and on their way back to El Paso.

"An arroyo some hundred yards distance was deep enough to conceal myself and my steed. From there I was able to spy the top of the mesa through some brush on the lip. The monster flew fast, I was unable to see it until the moonlight showed it on the top of the cottonwood tree under which you waited. When it landed, I climbed out and crawled my way to a distance I thought I could hit the beast when it made ground. We are fortunate it stopped right off instead of charging at you."

Walker nodded. "I called out its name before it could move. That's what caused it to freeze long enough for us both to shoot."

"So, the legends are true."

"It so appears."

The second day after they killed the Skinwalker found Cheyenne Walker and Miss Kitty Belle once again in The Holed Ace saloon. This time they weren't against the wall away from the bar, but seated on high stools behind it, next to Judge Jim Bean and Sheriff Ken Goode. Most of the farmers and sheep owners who'd been there before were also crowded into the room. Newspaperman Billy Locke was against the far wall, as were Sergeant Malakai Grant and three of his Buffalo Soldiers.

"This here meeting of the El Paso Shepherds Association will now come to order!" the judge roared as he hammered his gavel on his block of wood. "The bar is closed until after the meeting, and I don't want to hear any complaining about it. You knew coming in that the bar would be closed as soon as the meeting came to order, so if you don't have your drinks now, that's your own fault. Now," he turned to Walker and Kitty Belle, "I understand you have something to tell us." He gestured at them to begin.

"Yessir," Kitty Belle said. "Thank you, your Honor. Aided by Mr. Cheyenne Walker, and with information from Mr. Tal Merca the sutler, we deduced that the killings were perpetrated by the Navajo shaman Yeitso." She nodded at Walker, who picked up the narrative.

"When Tal Merca told us that the Mescalero expelled him when he treated them the same way he had whites and Mexicans here, we figured it was him and devised a trap."

"Which was successful," Miss Kitty said. "The Navajo medicine man Yeitso is dead, and the attacks on lone cowboys and depredations on your sheep are now in the past."

"You have a question, Mr. Locke?" Judge Bean said when the newspaperman waved his hand.

"Yessir, I do. What about the rumor that Yeitso was a Skinwalker? Did you find any truth to that?"

Walker and Miss Belle exchanged a glance, then she said, "As Sergeant Grant assured us, Skinwalkers are merely Indian superstition."

"Besides," Walker said, "would you have believed us if we said he was?"

A susurration of negatives rode through the crowd.

"There you have it," Kitty Belle said.

"Where's the body?" someone shouted.

"As soon as Yeitso was dead, buzzards and coyotes began descending on the remains. We chose not to contest with them and left the body where it was being devoured," Walker answered.

"Does anybody else have something to add?" Judge Bean asked. "If not, I declare this meeting ended and the bar open. Mr. Sasper, a glass of your best top-shelf whiskey, if you please?"

ABOUT THE AUTHOR

DAVID SHERMAN, AGED 78, PASSED AWAY QUIETLY IN THE company of his friends and loved ones on November 16, 2022, in Ft Lauderdale, Florida, due to prolonged health complications. He was born on February 27, 1944, in Niles, Ohio. He joined the Marine Corps out of high school and served in Vietnam. From April 1966 to September 1966, he was a squad leader with Combined Action Platoon and received numerous medals and citations. After leaving active service, David moved to Philadelphia where he attended the Pennsylvania Academy of the Fine Arts, becoming, for a brief time, an award-winning sculptor.

In 1983, David began his writing career with the novel *Knives in the Night*, published by Ivy Books, a division of Ballantine Books. He would go on to write over thirty novels, including the best-selling Starfist and Starfist: Force Recon series and the Star Wars novel *Jedi Trial* with co-author Dan Cragg, and his solo series, DemonTech. His short fiction appeared in Weird Trails, the award-winning Defending the Future series, and the award-winning Bad-Ass Faeries anthologies. Much of his fiction drew on his combat experience. For years, David was a fixture at many east coast science fiction conventions, including Philcon and Balticon.

His books have been translated into Czech, Polish, German, and Japanese.

In his later years, he found it difficult to continue to write about war, focusing instead on weird western and steampunk short fiction, but with the help of author Keith R.A. DeCandido he did complete his original novel series The 18th Race trilogy (*Issue In Doubt, In All Directions*, and *To Hell and Regroup*). In a nod to those who served, every character mentioned in the series was named after a recipient of the Medal of Honor.

Sherman's Last Stand, a collection of his steampunk short stories, will be published posthumously by eSpec Books, under their Paper Phoenix Press imprint.

David is survived by his siblings, Bev Taylor, Robert Towles, Mary Carano, and their respective families. He leaves behind many friends and fans to give tribute to his memory.

www.ingramcontent.com/pod-product-compliance
Lightning Source LLC
Chambersburg PA
CBHW030804190726
48285CB00003B/1009